Secret Thoughts

Sensual and quirky flash fiction with a twist

Renate van Nijen

ISBN 978-90-815393-1-9

Published by Palcho Publications
email: renate@renate-kunst.nl
website: www.renate-kunst.nl

With special thanks to Jennifer Griffiths and Sandra Kramer

Table of contents:

Artwork by Renate van Nijen:

The artwork on the cover, '**Secret Thoughts**', (oil on canvas), very much represents the content of the short stories and flash fiction.

Most of the stories are about relationships described through an inner sensing, intuition and sensual feeling in the belly, which becomes an eye to view the world.

Renate's art can be viewed on www.renate-kunst.nl

The man and the barmaid

She's radiant as she distributes orders from the shiny tray. He finds her so clever the way she carries six plates laden with food in her left hand, leaving her right hand free to serve, without a trace of self-doubt, her beautiful, somewhat tired face reflected in his eyes. Hers are blue, with the type of clarity that gives you butterflies in your stomach. He knows that, because he feels it, now, here. She is special, elusive, and he would love to take hold of her. Her medium-length blonde hair falls loosely around her face. She is friendly and helpful, always a smile to share and a pleasant voice, creating a certain intimacy, as if she is only there for him.

She leans forward while her warm voice asks what she can do for him. That, of course, he knows only too well. He tries not to stare too obviously at her breasts which, for a short moment, allow him an exciting view.

He orders a cappuccino which she serves him with a small glass of whisky liqueur topped with an elegantly twisted blob of cream. He loves that, almost as much as he loves her, but that is his secret. A secret which he finds difficult to hide from her. He carefully slides the two sugar cubes from the saucer into the frothy head of his coffee. Slowly they disappear into the creamy mass. He enjoys the coffee so skilfully prepared by her. He forces himself to avert his eyes because he doesn't want her to feel uncomfortable under his gaze, as uncomfortable as he himself feels, hopping around on his bar stool, trying to look indifferent. His self-confidence is wavering. Feeling rather silly, wondering whether she suspects anything. He almost wants her to. Automatically his mind starts to work overtime. With an almost suggestive gesture he picks up the cup which contains one last shot of cappuccino and brings it to his lips, scrutinizing her. He becomes aroused as he surreptitiously examines her body when she isn't paying attention to him, yet must subconsciously know that he is staring at her. The curves of her body clearly defined in the low-cut white blouse and the tight jeans under a long dark blue cotton apron.

He knows that she will never be his for the asking, so he takes her into a dark, unmentionable corner of his mind.

Not analyzing makes it somehow less sinful, so with saliva gathering in his mouth he imagines her wearing only that long apron open at the back and unwittingly giving him a glimpse of her beautiful cheeks ... cheeks that he would love to sprinkle with some scented oil and rub, quickly pushing them apart, kissing them. He asks her for a serviette which she gives him with a professional smile that he wants to believe is just for him. He is grateful to her and again takes her to that dark corner of his mind where she is suddenly willing and gladly does what he asks of her. He sees how she enjoys herself passionately with a Lolita-like glint in her adult eyes, seducing him slowly and provocatively as she undresses. Shamelessly she moves towards him, takes his hands and slides them over her body, touching her hips, her beautiful round buttocks, her undulating abdomen and her breasts. Looking deeply into his eyes, smiling and telling him that all is well. He imagines that he can smell her. A warm, almost musky fragrance. He kisses her on the neck, wraps his arms around her and pulls her gently against him. He feels the spasms in her lower body which she teasingly moves back and forth. He trembles slightly and realizes that it is time to go.

Clumsily he pays for the cappuccino with some loose change and, hopefully, a smile not too aroused. He realizes that his excitement has reached his lower body. He quickly heads home where he discharges his self-made joy of life into the serviette which she had so kindly given him earlier.

Shit! .... not strong enough!!!

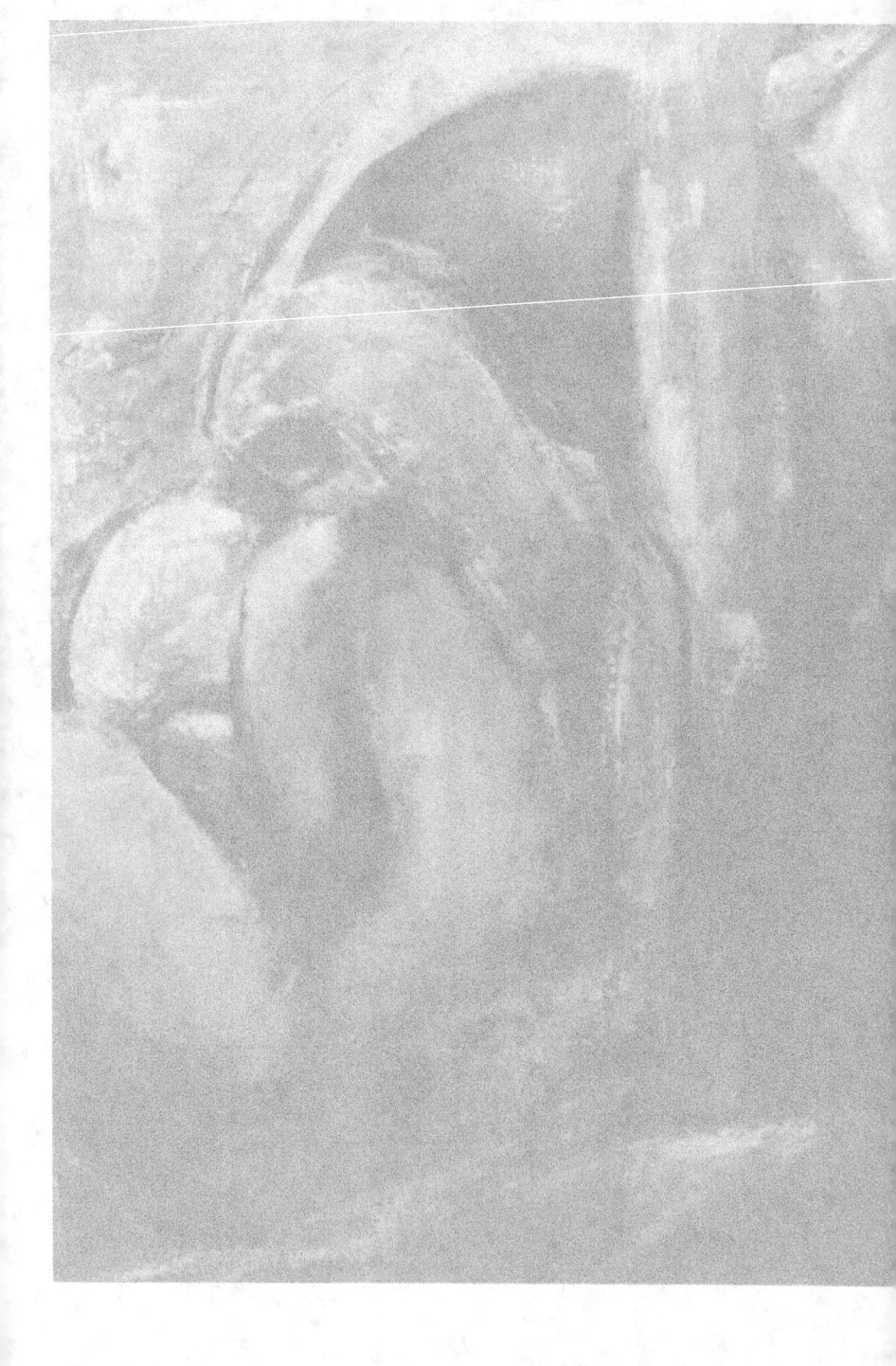

Passing by

The weather was beautiful, the sun was shining and a cool breeze made the temperature pleasant. Sitting in the low windowsill in front of the open window in a cosy student house in the city centre, she felt somewhat melancholy. Unable to understand why even though she felt good, she still dragged along this slumbering feeling of sadness. She poured herself another cup of green tea and watched the activity in the street beneath her. The owner of the café on the corner of the street placed four tables and chairs on the narrow pavement for guests to enjoy the lovely springtime sunshine. Clothes shops opened their doors so that fresh air could drive out the rather musty winter atmosphere. It seemed as if everyone was wearing smiles on their faces. A happy Saturday morning. The wonderful weather the reason why summer clothes had been taken out of attics. Frivolous dresses in lively colours, t-shirts with loud slogans, fashionable nail polish on toes happily peeking out of flip-flops and sandals. All this made the sunny scene even more intense.

Daydreaming, staring down into the street, she saw that the tables of the café were occupied by a group of students who, just a bit too noisily, embroidered their nocturnal adventures in word and gesture. Love was in the air, bellies full of butterflies. She decided to go for a walk in the park not far from her house. Her warm charisma, messily held up dark blonde hair, wide green linen trousers and a tight white cotton t-shirt with a deep v-neck caused a few passionate stares here and there. She did not notice them; she was in deep thought as she strolled along. It was the end of May, the ground was strewn with blossom and leaves on the trees deepened their green colour. She loved this time of year. Everything started to wake up and people were in the mood for life. She felt her melancholic mood disappearing and inhaled the delicious spring fragrance. It was fairly quiet in the park. Some joggers in sweaty lycra, an elderly woman with a funny sausage dog, and a lot of lively birds enhanced the atmosphere.

Then she saw him, almost unconsciously, more or less in passing by. He was so big and strong. A symbol of strength. She wanted to touch him, to be absorbed by him, let him become absorbed by her, talk to him. Lean against him. He was beautiful. He looked like the others but was nevertheless special, she sensed it. She felt the energy flowing through her veins, aware of every step she made, quite nervously, because she knew that she would give in to her feelings. She felt a strong urge to stop.

They did not really look at each other and yet there was an attraction, strongly present in such a way that she could not possibly ignore it. A little shy she walked towards him, stopped for a moment when she was very close, doubtful. He did not seem to mind. She looked around, to convince herself that nobody was paying any attention to her and she felt excited, knowing she was going to do something forbidden which would make her feel alive. She slowly walked further and now she was so close that she could touch him. He smelled of spring. She touched him, carefully as if it were not allowed. Feeling his strength, looking up to him, in a pleasant way. She knew that he would protect her. Full of desire she started to talk to him. Trying to explain why she needed him. Why she wanted to borrow him for a moment, use him, absorb his wisdom. She did not even expect an answer. She heard it nevertheless. She leaned against him. Pushed her body against his powerful base. Immediately she felt agitation and satisfaction at the same time. She wrapped her arms around him and was no longer aware of anything else. She felt how his hard trunk used her body. He had everything within him, male, female, life and death. Indestructible and weak. His energy and power seemed to run through her. She felt protected, grand and yet humble. She felt one with him, one with nature and one with herself. The answer was within her. Her melancholic mood had disappeared. She just stood there, satisfied and happy, leaning against him for a while, enjoying his wonderful gifts.

He looked down on her, somewhat bored. Of course he had heard her. He had heard them all for years, many years. They came to him for strength and energy, they who believed in him. That was a rather pleasant feeling, the amount of knowledge that he could give others. He thought back to how it had all started for him. It wasn't easy. Like so many he still carried the roots of his past. The first years had been the most difficult. Working himself up through the dark towards the light. But also in the light there were many dangers awaiting him. He had defied a lot of storms, overcome them all. Meanwhile he had grown old and wise, seen everything and no longer felt the need to prove himself. He knew he was an important source for many. Through him they could breathe, but he also gave them strength and a zest for living. And today he met her. She was beautiful, strong but also vulnerable. He scattered a blanket of his shade around her. He knew he gave her strength, but he was also captured by her passion, feeling attracted to her in a strange way. She was special, different from many others who had preceded her. She gave something back, only by being who she was. He looked around and saw the beauty of nature, of life, and realised that not only could he give, but also receive. It gave him a good feeling. And with due pride he shook his green top and dropped a leaf ... right on the tip of her nose.

In pieces

She was made in a moment of pure love, perfect collaboration, an enthusiastic togetherness, sparkling. Scorching heat. The man who created her a satisfied, very experienced man, happy with his daily existence. He had done it so often that it had become part of his being. At 17 he had his first experience. That was incredibly exciting. It certainly wasn't easy. He remembered it as if it were yesterday. Walking into the room where it was going to happen. He knew it, but it was nevertheless somewhat unreal, hard to grasp. It was hot, very hot. He felt terribly awkward and, to be honest, it was not really satisfactory. But an inexplicable urge within made him want to do it again and again, becoming experienced. He wanted more and so he regularly returned to that exciting place, addicted to the heat, the smells and the sparkles which were always abundantly present. He became passionate and could do what he loved doing most, forged with love.

The road she had walked to get where she was had not always been easy. She could exert little influence on that. Everything was decided for her. There was light and darkness in her life. Often she found herself with others in a small dark space with little partitions, somewhat musty. That was ghastly. Although she was handled with care, there were moments she felt locked up, falling prey to the will of others. The place of her destination dependent on chance which might be better described as destiny. She had learned to accept what she could not change. Yet she knew that she was lucky.

She has been here for some time now. In front of a mirror in a cosy space. She shines beautifully and has become narcissistic because of this forced confrontation with her own image. She is rather exceptional, not average at all. She has beautifully round shapes and is special compared to others of her kind, for this reason she stands in this special spot. Visible to everyone, but safe, not vulnerable. She is quite proud of that. She likes to be special. Like he is special to her. He is a regular, comes several times a week. She waits for him, every evening. She wants to make him happy, and from experience she knows she can. She loves the blissful expression on his face when she is with him. He comes in and she hopes that he will choose her again. She thinks he is beautiful with his short blond hair and his clear blue eyes. She likes it when those eyes are looking at her. She would love to be his, and only his, but she has no choice. So she reconciles herself with the situation and fantasises about him.

Today he is here and that makes her happy. He looks at her, asking for her as he often does. He takes her to his table with a view out over the square, full of bars and restaurants.

There are stalls with glittering objects that people can buy to give as a gift to someone dear to them. Only a few more weeks, then it will be Christmas. A nice time for those who are not alone, but not for her. She doesn't like Christmas. It always gives her an empty feeling, even though in fact at that time she is often literally full. She does not belong to anybody and that always makes her feel lonely.

But tonight she is happy because he is with her. He sits in front of her and looks at her. She feels a little uncomfortable, pleasantly uncomfortable. He touches her, feeling her cold exterior, but when he explores her, as so often, she will take on his warmth. She is willingly in his hands and becomes excited when he fills her with a cold substance which makes him feel happy within. The first drops are poured into her, the oxygen withdrawn from her. She starts to ogle him. She knows he wants her. Sparkling with excitement she feels how he picks her up, giving her the blissful sensation of flying. She sees how he moistens his lips with his tongue, carefully bringing her to his mouth, a nicely sculptured mouth with small creases. The soft colour of his lips gives her a great feeling, waiting for the moment they will touch her, longing for her inner beauty. When the moment is there she gives him everything she has. He smiles, looking at her.

Some time later he gets up, leaving her alone with the memory of the wonderful sensation she has just experienced. She wants to be near him, to belong to him for ever, and to be there for him when he needs her. She looks at him and hears him asking if he can take her home, if she can become his. He says that he has such special memories of her and wants to have her all to himself. She waits full of tension, full of hope. After some inaudible discussion he walks back to their table, smiles at her and whispers: "You are mine."

He carefully wraps a scarf around her and they walk out of the door. She is happily surprised by this unusual change in her existence. Not knowing where he will take her, but she doesn't mind. She feels safe, carried by him, wanted by him. Twilight is setting in and together they walk through the streets with the

Christmas lights. It is cold, but she doesn't feel it. He warms her, like she has warmed him so often.

After ten minutes they arrive at an old house along the canal, his house. They walk up the stately stairs; he opens the door and takes her in. Excited she wonders what will happen next. Once inside they go to the kitchen. He lights a couple of candles. The scarf falls on the ground and he takes her in his hands again, looks at her and fills her with the cold liquid he loves so much. She enjoys the ecstasy and as always she becomes wet inside. He drinks her, enjoys her, touches her with his mouth, that beautiful mouth. She welcomes his attention, his passion and his love for her. She shines and glitters in the candle light. He fills her again, with a white liquid, and takes her with him to his bedroom, not letting go of her. With restrained tension she waits for what will happen. With his free hand he takes off his clothes, somewhat impatiently. He has a beautiful body. He greedily enjoys her wetness again and lies down on the bed on his back, completely naked, playing with her. He rolls her over his body, from one side to the other, from top to bottom. They both feel that she is getting warm, a bit sticky. The ecstasy becomes blurred and suddenly she wonders why she wanted this so much. After some time he grabs her rather roughly and puts her down on the wooden floor next to the bed. She feels lonelier than ever in the darkness. The vague light of the table lamp doesn't cast its shine on her and she longs to be back in her spot in front of the mirror in the light. She looks up one last time and to her horror she sees his large feet coming towards her, not noticing her, breaking her into a thousand pieces.

Her life in shatters at his feet … it doesn't bother him now, but will it tomorrow?

The journey

Amsterdam: 7.15 am

Terrifying beauty. The sparkling of an early awakening sun on a visual sprawl of modern civilization. Disconcerting, also intensely wonderful and incomprehensible. Water, too many roads. I feel sick, a heavy feeling in my stomach, a little dizzy. A boy is chattering, his English so much better than mine. Everything is getting smaller and smaller. I try to recognize the unmistakable fear lying beneath the smiling faces of the holiday-makers surrounding me. There is also trust, complete faith. I don't understand it. So much weight; according to the law of gravity mine alone sufficient to come down rapidly and painfully. I am shivering but try to hide it for those who share my adventure. Nobody notices; each one of them wrapped in their own little world. I inhale deeply and calmly through my nose and exhale slightly longer through my mouth. It seems to help. Breath, a sign of life. That life that now seems so vulnerable. My life. I feel drawn to the magazine in the net on the back of the seat in front of me. Thumbing through the pages the words seem blurred. Shouting images in strong colours and words in bold text. Perfect men and women recommending unimportant things. My attention is grabbed by the girl with a silly hat, pinned crookedly onto her craftily sculpted bun, explaining some instructions which nobody seems to pay any attention to. Not actually expecting to really need them. That is something that happens to others, not to them, but I am the other. A hypochondriac, always thinking that everything will happen to me, worried about creating my own reality. So I must work really hard to think positively, everything is fine. I switch on my mp3 player. New age music fills my brain. Appropriate to die with ... 'partire è morire un po' ... I look out of the window and discover an endless blanket of white clouds reaching beneath a vague blue sky, a surreal horizon. I am looking for an angel, one of those who protect, preferably a few, so that they can take good care of me. I cannot see any but they are there. One has just reassured me, I can feel her smile; I know I amuse them. I want to roll in the clouds. I often want the impossible. I see scratches on the double glazing. I don't like scratches. Not in a place like this; here everything needs to be perfect. Everyone acts as if they think this is normal, so many people trapped in a thin layer of flimsy-looking material patched together with a few nuts and bolts, high above everything and everybody. Suddenly we change direction and for a moment I am dazzled by the sun, a pleasant feeling. Warm white flannels are handed out. I gratefully wipe the nervous drops of sweat off my face, neck and hands. I look around me, my head filled with mad thoughts. Shall I pull down the handle under the 'Exit' sign??? I don't like mad ideas, they are intrusive, entering my space uninvited. I shake them off. My eyes well up with tears. The beauty of the view stills me while the total lack of control freezes me. I am extremely aware of having a body, reminded by my insides. A vague headache, indigestible flatulence that makes me feel even heavier. I don't want to be heavy, never, but especially not here. I feel an unpleasant need to go to the smallest room, but I will not give in to that, here it is claustrophobically small. My thoughts drift off again and I look out of the tiny window. The blanket of clouds is inviting. I want to go there. I feel incredibly lonely. Wishing to be in the company of a good-looking man who I can grab. I will invent one. Together we listen to the music, sharing the headphone of my mp3. It is as if we belong together, as if we are one. We want more. He is beautiful, an omen for what lies ahead of me. Wavy black hair and a white shirt that shows off his tanned skin, his short beard dangerously attractive in his striking Italian face. He loves me, just like that. A castle is rising from the clouds. The castle where we will live. There is champagne ... lively bubbles. The sun warms me and works its magic. A realistic wing becomes a surreal, strange reality, reflecting the sun which scatters light over me, turning my hair into softly undulating golden curls. It is pleasantly warm in the castle. The sound of baroque music fills the room, the floor covered by a thick carpet of clouds, soft and gentle. I fall onto my back and he carefully pours some champagne over me. I am naked. It feels indescribably safe. He caresses my hair and carefully explores the shape of my face with the tips of his fingers. He cautiously bends forward towards me. His lips searching for mine, very gentle and yet extremely intense. He carefully licks the bubbles off my body. Mountain tops rise from the clouds. I am shaking. Everybody is shaking, but all is good. I even dare to enjoy myself. The blanket of clouds suddenly frail, breaking up in places. The rugged beauty takes my breath away; I'm attracted by the glittering in the clouds, deep down below me. Would that be one of my angels? I am sure it is. I feel excited but calm. I take a last glance at the lovely smile playing around his mouth.

The blanket has become a sheet, soft as silk. A white sea beneath a blue horizon. Am I the only one who can look at this for hours?

Roma 9.15 am. Ciao!

Valentine's Day

It all started when I asked myself: how sad can it get if a mere smile, OK, a nice one, takes you by surprise and suddenly words seem to get stuck in your throat, your favourite pizza becomes tasteless and you drop about 35 years in age, acting like a spotty adolescent ... which is exactly what happened to me a few months ago after my session with an acupuncturist, for no particular reason apart from keeping my energy in balance. After my treatment, still floating a little, I decided to go for a meal at my favourite Italian pizzeria. The waiter, a rather tiny Italian with a great nose gave me a smile from ear to ear as soon as he noticed me. I immediately became extremely nervous, totally undoing the perfect balance so carefully established by the acupuncture treatment. I felt very much alive, enjoying the unexpected admiration and butterfly sensation created in my belly, his smile turning me into a giggling creature with all sorts of too-long-forgotten sensations swirling through my body, making me lose my appetite. I felt shy under his attention, staring and smiling at me every time he walked in or out of the pizzeria to serve customers enjoying their Italian food on the outdoor terrace. Having totally lost the habit of flirting all I could do was reluctantly eat my pizza, trying not to spill a blob of tomato sauce on my white top, smiling back at him in as grown-up a manner as possible and instead of the conversation that I promised myself I would start when he asked if everything was according to my wishes, I answered 'Si grazie', with a squeaking, barely audible voice. If only he knew where I took him in my fantasy! As a result of this little adventure I walked around in a blurry state for about a week, totally ignoring trying to make a living. Presuming that my Italian waiter was around toy-boy age, a cheeky smile filled my brain and radiated from my face when I dared to go into my private made up world where life was exciting and thrilling, creating fluids in places that need no mentioning.

My energy was sizzling, my aura undoubtedly full of shiny sparkling colours which was confirmed by the second looks I got from people in the street when I ran around like a headless chick, not really knowing where I was going apart from in the direction of the sea to have a good stare and listen over and over again to the *Tarantella del gargano* by Gianni Lamagna, an impressive song from Naples.

Whether the Italian waiter, of whom I knew nothing and who could just as well be married, gay or a mass murderer, was in need of a woman with wet briefs remained to be seen. To get an answer to that question I had no choice but to act. So, I discussed away all the contras in my brain that seemed to make perfect sense, because a woman of my age can't, what will he think, it is not done, I might be rejected and where will that leave me, and decided to be braver than ever before taking advantage of the forthcoming Valentine's Day. Not capable of stringing a sentence together in his presence I chose a meaningful blank card and explained why his penetrating eyes and sexy smile made me too nervous to approach him directly, but if going out for a coffee with me would please him, I would be happy to hear from him and if not, he could consider the card as a compliment. On Valentine's Day I asked a friend to join me for a pizza at the cosy restaurant. Clearly pleasantly surprised by my appearance he came over to our table bearing his special smile, taking our order and greedily accepting my card.

The outcome was almost unimportant because the gift he unknowingly gave me was powerful and long-lasting thanks to the stormy affair that had already repeatedly taken place in the privacy of my head. I was nevertheless still secretly hoping for this adventure to become even more real than it already was in my mind. His 'ti chiamo' which means as much as 'I will call you' was gracefully welcomed by me with a broad smile and a twinkle in my eyes ...

Two months on and no longer expecting his call, the lively sensual images having faded away into the distance of my imagination, I have taken matters into my own hands and I am waiting for the postman to deliver my special package ... in plain brown paper, including batteries, ordered online.

The traffic jam

They say that life only really starts now. When I woke up this morning, still a little drowsy, I looked in the mirror and saw an attractive adult woman with a youthful charisma, a little naughty in fact. Searching for tiny wrinkles – I was quite amused to have found a few. I felt great and contrary to my usual habit I left home for work in the centre of Amsterdam more or less on time. Leaving 39 years behind I searched for the open door which now lay ahead of me, a smile on my face.

And now this! A traffic jam! The temperature is well above 30°C. When you drive with the car windows open it is fine, but not stationary in the full sun ... I feel some tiny drops of sweat trickle down my neck and décolleté which I can find quite sexy under different circumstances. I also feel some drops on my back, alternately slow and somewhat more rapid, moving in the direction of my lower back and I feel how the drops slide down to the soft inclination of my lower back and then disappear between my buttocks, quite a nice feeling. I am aroused. Uncertain whether it is because of the stress or the sensual impact of my own sweat, I decide to simply enjoy the moment.

All cars are now at a standstill. Mine is in the right lane and I look around. In my side mirror I see a right-hand-drive vintage car. I'm always curious about who would own a car like that and I take a discreet peek at the driver. Mmm, he is quite attractive. Black hair, slightly greying at the temples. Dark eyes and a friendly mouth. His tanned arm hangs somewhat nonchalantly from the window and I look at his graceful hand. I wouldn't mind a hand like that opening the clasp of my bra, carefully dividing the pearls of sweat over my back, gently massaging while he is standing behind me subtly pushing his lower body against mine, his hands slipping down via my neck and shoulders, slowly pushing down the straps. Those hands which, not too boldly, but discreetly are looking for and finding the curves of my breasts and mmmmm …

'One beep and a hoot is really more than enough … you fool!'. Through the rear view mirror I see the car behind me in which an elderly man is gesticulating angrily at me. He looks wild, his bloated face turned red to reveal that he has been drinking too much for many years. Yuck! What an annoying disturbance to my nice fantasy. I am disappointed that the cars in front of me slowly accelerate. The left lane now also slowly starts moving. My long hair has become wet with the excitement and heat. Cars crawl along, but we don't make much progress. The man in the vintage car passes me. I hardly dare to look at him. It is almost as if he knows that I experienced a sensual moment with him in my head. Crazy idea in fact, but also thrilling, to think that a good-looking guy does exciting things with you in his imagination! Oh dear, he is looking at me, slightly too penetratingly. My face turns red and I feel caught out but cannot suppress a smile, and I'm glad he has to drive on. By now we have already been driving slowly for 5 minutes. Then I see the row of cars next to me stop again. I realize that I will have to stop exactly next to him, I feel embarrassed. I can almost feel the warmth of his body. He is looking at me. We are now only half a metre apart, and could touch each other if we wanted. His steering wheel on the right, mine on the left. Sultry summer sounds come from his car, jazzy, not too complicated. Oh my God I cannot stop thinking about sex, hope he can't read my mind and look inside my head. I can feel and sense that he is looking at me. He also knows that I am watching him out of the corner of my eye. His face, like mine, beaded with sweat. I'd rather not think about how embarrassing the drops are that find their way from my forehead to my cleavage. He wets his lips. I know that he is aroused by me. I dare to look at him for a short moment. He looks at me. He absolutely has the most beautiful eyes that you would want to stare into on a sultry summer's day in a traffic jam. I sense that he finds me attractive as well. While he captures my stare, he briefly and sensually licks and kisses the inside of his hand, opens it and blows the wet kiss towards me. I grab it out of the air and quickly put it into my mouth. We both start laughing. He has a deep, sensual laugh and I know that my warm, slightly husky laughter has reached him as well, touching him in his lower parts. Something very special is happening. I know that his hand is finding its way to his trousers and he knows that my hand is finding its way to my briefs. I roll up my dress, a summer dress with dozens of small buttons, and inconspicuously open some of the top buttons. I caress my neck, the curves of my breasts, then a little lower. I know that he is looking at me and loves what I am doing. Carefully I move my left hand inside the dress to caress myself, almost wanting him to see my full breasts, but that is not possible. I move the dress a little further aside knowing that he can now see the rounding of my breasts and a tiny part of the dark skin of one of my nipples, slightly trembling. I am terribly excited. Meanwhile trickles of sweat run down my warm body, making it extra sensual. I just have to caress myself in other places and I know that he has also reached his intimate parts, thinking about me. A sweltering tension is created between both cars. From his facial expression I can see that he understands that I have also reached my most intimate spot. I open my legs, caress myself and feel the familiar warmth. A heightened sensual titillation takes possession of me and could release at any moment in an overwhelmingly delicious sensation. I quickly throw one more glance at the car next to me and see that he has also reached his peak at that very same moment. During my climax forgetting all about him, melting into the now. I lick my lips and blow a brief kiss back to my traffic jam lover. Then I realize that the cars in his lane have started moving again. He smiles, and I take that as a beautiful gift. Today I have become 40!

Inspiration

So many delicacies passing by on an ordinary Tuesday in April. I am in Amsterdam, buying a train ticket to Arnhem. It is ten o'clock in the morning and I am surprised at my interest in what is happening. Observing people I notice several stories waiting to be written, filling my head with inspiration. Unexpected events that I can re-write, mixing memories with a colourful reality, inspired by occasional passers-by. I look around me and see a diversity of people. A middle-aged woman walks in the direction of the platform; she wears a glittery black dress, far too tight, clearly showing off her body a little too loudly; staggering on platform-soled shoes which exaggerate her calves. The man who accompanies her kisses her gently on her mouth. I feel a twinge of jealousy, also longing for a gentle mouth. I watch a group of young men passing by. Finding them quite attractive, I quietly observe them without arousing suspicion. They feel so grown up, so adult. You can see that from the way they walk, all legs, coming from nowhere, going nowhere. Thinking they know it all, already strongly believing in their convictions, full of great intentions, dreaming about a beautiful future without real expectations. Hoping to be able to change the world. Not like their parents, who also once had ideals, but never understood anything. Parents who so dramatically tried to stay young.

I pay for the ticket with some loose change that I keep in a side-pouch of my camel-leather bag and walk onto the platform. I take a seat on a bench next to a neat elderly gentleman, who's leaning on a worn-out walking stick. He looks tired, a little worn out himself, without interest in his surroundings. I am observing and enjoy what I see. A young man walks past, short Rasta curls playfully adorning his head, happily wobbling. His beautiful brown eyes cast a quick look at mine, but I see no recognition. That makes sense, but I would have liked it to have been different. I cannot keep my eyes off him and wrestle with my indecent thoughts as I sit here on the platform waiting for the train, after my one-night stand with an attractive man.

I recall everything that we spoke about and everything that we had not thought of. Remembering when I wrote to him in response to his letter to me, in which he had enclosed a small photograph of himself, as requested in my personal ad in the newspaper. Trying to outline a picture of myself, chatting about things that interested me and the sport that I practise. Joyrobic. This is very happy aerobic or, at least, that is what the name seems to suggest, and was something that I did on a weekly basis in a small dull hall with several ladies in wide, pastel-coloured track suits, who would not feel at ease in aerodynamic outfits with a string between their cheeks. The truth was of course very frustrating. That a string in an anal cleft can actually be very handy during joyrobic because it will make you jump a little higher was not relevant to the ladies.

The small fat chihuahua on the platform warms my soul while I realise that her mummy loves her nevertheless and that beauty can be present in an unexpected angle.

I suddenly have to hurry to catch my train and am surprised

by the bustle. There is just one seat free opposite a young man who vaguely smells like trees, his hair hanging in his eyes, it's too long, but it makes him beautiful in a girlish way. I look at his profile from the corner of my eye, with greed, while the train starts moving. The sun is shining. My head is filled with sentences that seem logical at this moment. I decide to relax and rest my head against the back support of the seat. A sexy, loud girl almost drowns out the sound of the racing train. A cow looks up, bored, used to the drifting clouds. I doze off, then return to reality when the train stops at Utrecht. Passengers come and go. I see that the young man in front of me has fallen asleep. The train starts moving again and some rays of sunlight cast through the window onto his face. He is terribly young, in his early twenties, so much younger than I am, but he fascinates me when I look at his long eyelashes and remind myself of the beauty of living. He is not aware of my eyes resting on him. I look at his mouth; it hangs slightly open while his head leans against the seat. It is a kind mouth. I look at his lips … they are full and gorgeous, gently inviting, nicely wet and innocent. I really want to lick them, make careful gentle movements with the tip of my tongue. I feel a bit naughty but I just have to make a move, take a step … a step towards him on my high heels that make me feel really feminine. Carefully I bend forward in his direction. Even more carefully I lick his beautiful lips and sense the briny taste of drowsy youth. Just as I want to further discover his youthful inside with my tongue he opens his eyes. He looks at me and I feel caught, as if he can read my thoughts, as if he knew what I had done with him in my head. I smile timidly.

The train comes to a standstill at Arnhem station. He quickly takes his coat and gets off the train … I get off as well and walk along the platform, feeling a little melancholic. A secret encounter. The words that I would write ... inspired again. I see him walking ahead of me and just when I call myself back to reality he turns around and winks at me.

Olé, Olé, Olé ... Oh no!

Tonight he is going to have a good time. The football match of the year, England v Germany. The street and the houses are covered with English flags. England has to win of course. He is really looking forward to it, watching the match together with three of his mates at his place. He just has an hour or so to get some late shopping. Realizing that he has to hurry, he jumps into his red Ford Fiesta and drives slightly too fast to the supermarket. He quickly grabs a trolley and is glad that it is not too busy. He wonders what to buy for this evening. A tray of lager and a bottle of whisky, so that they can celebrate heavily or drown their sorrows. He looks around for crisps, frozen pizzas and French bread. 'OUCH! ... shit.'

'Sorry, oh sorry!' Her 'sorry' came from a full sensual mouth with a nice warm tone, the 'r' rolled deeply in the back of her throat, a little hoarse, a pleasant sensual sound. He had seen her before in the supermarket and found her terribly attractive. That messy curly red hair. The heart-warming freckles in her low, but not indecent, décolleté. Her exciting bosom. Those swaying full hips and the narrow waist.

Her lovely body bumps into him just like that and now a 'sorry' from her gorgeous mouth. And those eyes, so green! She squints a little which makes her sexy and exciting, somewhat intangible! She smiles, confused, which gives him a glance of the dimple in her right cheek. Nonchalantly, nervously, she runs her beautifully shaped hand through her hair. Something strange is happening; he does not know what to say. His head runs wild and he cannot make sense out of the many words which jostle one another on the back of his tongue. He is trembling on his feet. His throat is dry and he is frightened that his voice will squeak and creak when he talks to her. He knows he has to say something, anything, in reaction to her 'sorry', but he wants to tell her how beautiful she is. In fact he wants to grab her and tear her clothes off that wonderful body. Touching it with experience and appropriate love, taking those lovely warm breasts in his hands, caressing them, firmly, then gently again, teasing her. His hands full on her round bottom, pulling her against him so that their breathing stops, to then resume again, excited, warm and deep, while producing soft panting sounds. Body heat mixed with bodily fragrances. Carefully but nevertheless boldly kissing her on that beautiful full mouth. *Oh no, what am I doing? ... pffff.* He feels that he is just standing there, smiling a bit awkwardly, shrugging his shoulders. Seconds seem like hours and in response to her 'sorry' his mouth forms the words 'Oh, don't worry', but there is no sound. He feels totally uncomfortable, like an adolescent, timid and at the same time naughty. She is also frozen to the spot, lowering her eyes and looking at him mischievously, somewhat confused. Her long lashes mysteriously form a gentle, almost tangible shadow under her eyes. They are standing very close and he can feel the warmth of her body. Her hands are trembling and she fiddles awkwardly with the chain of the lock on her trolley. He thinks he is going crazy, but he has to touch her. All reason is gone and carefully he puts his hand on hers. He gets a shock. She notices it, not pulling away her hand. He caresses the blond hairs on her pale skin and is becoming aroused. She knows it as well. It seems to amuse her; her eyes are sparkling and a cheerful smile graces her lips. She wets them while she looks at him from beneath her long lashes. Waves of pleasure screech through his body and he takes a step towards her so that he can feel her soft body against his. He realizes that she feels his agitation. She recoils slightly, moving back her head so that her long hair playfully brushes his cheek, sighing, enjoying herself, just like him. He turns his head in such a way that he carefully touches her cheeks with his lips, she smells delicious, like limes, it doesn't matter that he doesn't even know how they smell. He wants to whisper in her ear: 'You are so beautiful, you excite me, I want you. I love your smell, I am falling in love with your curls, I want to explore you, love you.' She breathes heavily and he feels the tension. Time no longer exists. He vaguely realizes that he is in a supermarket and why he is there, but only this moment is important. Then, from the corner of his eye, he sees two young girls behind the cheese counter giggling at them. It takes him back to this beautiful reality and he senses everything even more intensely than before. He lets go of her arm and takes a small step back. He smiles at her and she smiles back at him. Then he clears his throat and says: 'I think you are wonderful, I would like to see you again, would you like to go out for a drink with me? May I give you my phone number?'

She opens her charming mouth and says: 'Wie bitte?'

Free as a bird

Three-dimensional nonsense, too much explanation, whereas what pops up in my head makes sense. Too much noise, almost annoying. Cyclists being blown away with the wind. Free as birds. They don't see much, hair playing in front of their eyes, a pleasant feeling in their faces. The wind creating a fresh soft feeling as if a gentle force can be pleasant. Flapping umbrellas, sweeping coats, dancing leaves. A flying hat. I decide to sit in it. The hat takes me to an unknown destination where I will never arrive, perhaps that is him. I feel embraced, encased in a cocoon loosely spun around me, leaving my spirit free, making me whole, complete again. I feel an exciting sensation, discovering sensuality in everything that is, nature, myself. I absorb it, allowing the feeling into my pores. The hat takes me along. A flock of birds flies in the sky, they are very close, I can almost touch them. Their beauty so powerful. Where are they going? I decide that they are leaving. Suddenly the wind subsides and the hat ends up in a red convertible. The sun starts shining, warming me. I feel total happiness and look around. The car is parked in front of a high hedge. If beauty lies hidden in a rocking branch with red berries, then where am I?

In the rear mirror I see a casually draped white pullover on the back shelf. The mirror shows a limited world, but when I watch long enough I discover more and the restricted world becomes spectacular. A brightly coloured bird secretly nibbles on a berry.

Someone approaches the car. He is roughly attractive. A pleasant Mediterranean look with a carefully created nonchalant short beard beneath his bright blue eyes, which, strongly contrasting with his dark curly hair, stare dreamily into the distance. He puts the hat on his head. I feel his messy curls and smell his freshly washed hair. He carries me along to the station and takes a seat in a stationary train. He puts the hat on the small table.

I look out of the window and see a salamander escaping between the pavement slabs on the platform. The sun intensifies its bright green colour, touching me in my belly, almost tangible. The train slowly starts moving. There is an ocean of sunflowers. I want to dive in, have a swim, inspired. I am an artist and take in the yellow glow of the sunflowers.

Small picturesque medieval villages lie along the track in the hills and grant me a view of a time past, too obviously present to be pushed away by the overwhelming sound of the pounding hip-hop music coming from the windows of a shiny black car waiting at the railway crossing. In spite of the speed of modern times, life seems to stand still. I go along in the peace and quiet and feel satisfied and happy. In the distance the blue-grey silhouette of a mountain chain, fossilized in time, dominantly present within my view. It stills me.

At the next station he picks up the hat, puts it on his head and gets off the train. He leaves the small station and crosses the square, sitting down at a wooden table outside a café in the small village. A few cyclists wipe the hair out of their faces and park their bicycles against the age-old olive tree in the middle of the square. He orders a glass of wine.

I crawl out of the hat; I'm an exciting energy. I don't feel lonely because I know I am part of a whole, realising that I am a cloud, floating above the hilly landscape. It's freedom, and while I swell up into a dark wet substance, I decide to come down in the form of a sensational drop, full of tension, warm and at the same time refreshing and exciting. I want him to recognise me and make sure he will notice. With a well-aimed landing, splashing slightly, overwhelming and very present I land on his nose. I see that he is startled and shakes me off, with regret because subconsciously he is aware of my sensuality. I end up in a colourful cane chair and suddenly he notices me. He starts talking and his voice is deep and warm. I want to suck on it, but decide to take it into my ears and it becomes a memory.

I look inside myself, distracted by the confusion in my throat and lower body. I can see the tension that I am feeling, my fast beating heart. Blood running through my veins faster than usual, nervous beating in my solar plexus. I recognise the symptoms of attraction, of falling in love which will dominate my life for a brief moment or for ever. I sense a vibration in my lower belly, warm waves taking away my breath, inadvertently flowing through my body. I am aware of my entire being, consisting of only energy, now so realistically present, like a fire. A fire of love and passion and the desire to love and be loved. I feel feminine and attractive. Leaving behind daily worries about inadequacies in a non-existent past.

He is extremely attractive, looking deep into my eyes, asking if I want to come with him, to hide in a tree house. We both laugh and he takes my hand; it feels familiar. I suddenly know that I belong to him and so does he. We climb into the tree and sit down on a colourful carpet in the tree house. He pulls me towards him and puts his arm around me. We look around us in silence. We can see the sea, blue as it should be, a little wild and pleasantly moving. We can hear the waves rolling over the colourful pebbles on the beach, soothingly ... shhhhhsss, shh-hhss ... creating a wonderful romantic melody together with the rustling of the leaves in the tree. After some time the compact clouds disappear, making space for a beautiful veil which hangs in the sky like an invitation. Pink, almost lilac, behind a gentle wall of light turquoise, very intense. A few floating clouds pass by, like an enormous hammock. Birds fly, allowing themselves to be guided, touching the careful clouds. We also want to enter that wondrous world. He gives me the confidence and together we take the plunge, falling onto a soft veil, sensual, with a natural intensity of passion. He takes me into his arms, softly kissing me. Looking for me with his wet tongue, from my mouth to my ear, my neck, further discovering my body. I hear the softly groaning, sweet sounds from deep down inside him and he whispers ... I need you. I understand what he means. My hands explore his body, recognizing it and giving myself to him, sharing. He helps me to feel free in my body. His touch changing me into a magic ball of emotions. Alternating between warm, goose pimples, wet, electric and shockingly uncontrollable. I enjoy him as much as he enjoys me, absorbing the smells that belong to him, never to forget them.

I feel more beautiful than ever and totally fuse with him, unifying with the clouds, never feeling lonely again. I realise that I am part of a whole. He knows it too. He looks up into the sky where he sees a bird flying. That is me, with a smile, free ...

When cultures meet

'I love big bellies and pale skin, and I love your soft long curly hair ... you are so, so beautiful,' he said with a strong accent.

He saw me dancing in the discothèque, during a perfect sweltering sensual evening filled with ethnic sounds where I enjoyed flaunting my Rubenesque body. I saw him watching me, I didn't mind, allowing the music to take me to a different place where I was happy, where I did not worry about the opinions of others, not even about my own. Dancing to sensual rhythms from every part of the world, alone, no need of a dance partner, comfortable in my Indian clothes, my body moving freely, without rules, without restrictions. No salsa or samba but funky low-beat sounds, my body undulating in waves. Wisps of long wet hair playing around my face, a glow on my skin, completely immersed in the music, free as a bird and seemingly unapproachable and mysterious yet open and strongly connected to the earth.

Suddenly he was there, right in front of me. Neat black hair and a fashionably shaped vague beard and moustache. Expensive up-market clothes and shoes with shiny buckles. Clearly quite a few years younger than me. I was intrigued, there was something that fascinated me and it wasn't just his large, almond-shaped light brown eyes. His dancing revealed his Eastern culture, crossing his legs at the sound of drums, his arms in the air, his fingers clicking, penetrating my eyes with a sensual look, captivating my attention. 'You are soooo beautiful,' he mimed. I was amazed but flattered by his interest. Whilst the sounds of music carried me beyond time, my inner sensation was lifted to a sensual level, like an intimate moment with a lover. One of many with him to come, but I didn't yet realize that. I felt attracted by him, but not enough so I promised only friendship.

A phone number on a frayed piece of paper. I decided to ring him after a few weeks. We met at the riverside on a day filled with sunshine and talked about the view that caressed our eyes, about rays of sun, creating a surreal scene with dancing gulls. We talked about freedom in our souls, the beauty of thoughts. An inspiring conversation. He stripped me with his eyes and with the right words, giving me the attention I so longed for.

We met regularly and I learned about his amazing life and culture. An Assyrian refugee from Iraq, part of an ancient, once important people, now without a country to call their own. A Christian with the facial features of a Muslim. I was fascinated by his stories, his experience in jail and his forgiveness when he expressed to me that nobody was all bad. I was humbled by the tolerance in his voice when he explained that after having been released from prison he saw the most cruel officer absolutely soft and gentle with his presumed grandchildren in a square in Baghdad. His younger years had been so intense that he had become wiser than me in many ways.

When I needed a comforting friend he was there. I appreciated his company, his amicable chit-chats about the sensual side of life and his compliments which made me smile. I fell for him long before I realised it, but he already knew. That is why he could wait. Until that special day. He was sitting next to me, sharing a sad moment in my life, putting his arms around me, allowing tears to run freely down my face. It was an intimate moment and I took fright when, through my grief, I sensed myself becoming aroused by him and my body almost unnoticeably and uncontrollably moved slightly in his direction so that his arm brushed unintentionally against my breast, within my personal space. Our friendship suddenly intimate. I decided to surrender to the desire, relaxing into the moment. I put my head on his shoulder and felt him stroking my hair. Then I took his hand and guided it inside my blouse, allowing him to feel the softness of my breast, very much aware of his tension and surprise. He responded with a tender touch and took my face in both his hands, wiped the tears off my cheeks and looked into my eyes, searching for approval; he could read me without words. Carefully he kissed my lips, waiting for me to react. I did, completely. He was so gorgeous, full of passion and yet initially a little clumsy. I suddenly felt incredibly safe in his arms. He smelled delicious and his beautifully shaped mouth was a pleasure to kiss. I was happy for him to be in control, allowing myself to be carried by his fantasy. He slowly took off my clothes, caressing every inch of my body, more skilful than I had ever experienced, telling me how beautiful I was. I melted in his sweet words and watched him taking off his clothes, revealing his slim but very strong body. Black hair covered his chest in a beautiful design, as if carved by a master. The touching of our bodies seemed so natural, so necessary, so meant to be. He was caring yet greedy, gentle yet intense. Slowly, yet full of passion, we discovered our bodies through our six senses. I felt beautiful and loved. His hands confidently found their way to my intimate parts where his soft yet secure touch was more than I could wish for and I opened myself up to him, gave him my everything, and fell in love with his sincere soul.

Evenings and days full of passion, of making love, of getting to know each other.

I was fascinated by his secrets, drawn into his world, realizing how different and yet welcome I was during the monthly festivals celebrating the Assyrian culture. But I did not really fit in. I knew he was only visiting my life for a short period of time and that we were not meant to be together for ever. I decided to enjoy the months we were given and forgave him his convenient lies when he chose to be with women from his own culture. It was OK. I knew we had to part.

And the day came when he met his Assyrian wife to be, a beautiful young woman from a different class to his which was clearly an impossible love in the context of Assyrian rules and traditions, but he was too sexually drawn in and could not see the warning signs. He moved on back to his culture, leaving me to move on into my future, with beautiful memories that I cherish like a secret that nobody will ever understand. Away from him, on the path which lay before me.

Two years later the phone rang: 'Hi, I cannot stop thinking of you ... you were right, I made a mistake ... Do you still have that soft beautiful long hair?? ...'

Yesterday

Observing the observing people so familiar to me, in the Grand Café. My own behaviour reflected in strangers. Looking like someone I don't want to look like. Judging matters which will leave my thoughts within minutes, making space for three young girls with their hair rolled in neat buns, wearing shoes with heavy platform soles dangling from their skinny legs, who just came in to disturb my peace, inspiring me at the same time. They smell of oranges, but that is nonsense of course, because some oranges have just been squeezed at the request of a bespectacled man with grey hair who is reading the newspaper. The girls take off their jackets and scrape some coins together, just enough for hot chocolate with cream, and put a pack of cigarettes on the table in front of them. My past acted out. They like to be grown-up, to be part of the adult world. A waiter with squeaky shoes. Body language that explains a lot. He can be delicious if he wants to be, he has an attractive nose. Exciting, I like classically shaped noses and become aware of a warm twinge in my lower body. I imagine that the squeaking shoes come towards me and that his hands touch mine insolently, impertinently, driving me crazy, while I nonchalantly try to unravel the hallucinations in my head, painfully aware of where I am. The shining steel of the six hand pumps glows in my face, reflecting it, deformed, exactly as I feel quite often, as right now, not entirely myself.

A lonely Sunday evening. Country music not too loud in my ear. Fortunately. I prefer the murmur of voices which I don't want to understand. I order a whisky to block out my somewhat awkward feeling, the awkward feeling of going out on my own in a society where it is still a little weird for a woman to do so. That is how it feels. Weird. I look around me and observe. Spectacles making ears stick out and a burning cigarette on a black ashtray. A young girl who doesn't lift up her feet when she walks by, otherwise she is vaguely beautiful. My round glass on the square coaster on the modern plastic bar comforts me. A coming and going of coffee-drinkers and people who stay to consume several alcoholic drinks. All welcome in this sociable get-together of strangers. Just another 15 minutes or so. If I were already considering going out on my own every now and then, I would carefully reconsider it. I suddenly feel uncomfortable and take a sip of my whisky. A few drops drip back into the glass, somewhat lethargically, playing a beautiful game with the melting ice cubes. It reminds me of blowing bubbles, sensual bubbles exploding without sound, touched by the wind on a warm summer's day in a forest near a small lake, whilst in the midst of foreplay, an intimate moment with the waiter. The reality less exciting. Friends with full agendas. Only one ticket for the Italian movie in the Alternative Cinema. And now a drink in my favourite bar. Touched by the words coming into my mind. Upended glasses, doing what they do best, glowing and shining. A mirror that reflects my face; I don't want to look at it, I am too tired. The country music becomes soporific. Of course I notice them, the great phrases, words originating from brains clouded by alcohol or drugs. Too beautiful to forget, too difficult to remember because in the end it doesn't really matter. Late-evening intellectuals trying to persuade each other of the beauty and sadness of life. The space absorbs the words and brings them to the head of the next visitor with an accidentally accessible ear. An involuntary listener who doesn't necessarily want to become any wiser. Words caught in the murmur. Valuable insights which will be forgotten tomorrow, possibly to be rediscovered once again in the brain of a wildly gesticulating young man, fogged by alcohol, who I have never seen before. I am not interested any more, pay for my drink and go home. Glad that tomorrow, today will be another yesterday.

The curtain

With a watery look in my emerald green eyes, looking away, feeling caught, because I know that he saw the curtain move. A moving event. I do it sometimes. Peeping, a quick look and then rapidly moving away or acting as if I have not seen someone. A bit painful, because deep down inside I know that this person has seen me as well. Not always in the mood to talk, rather being alone with my own thoughts, in my own world, as right now. My luxuriant ginger hair falls happily on my shoulders. I bare my snow-white teeth, dazzlingly smiling at me, reflected in the window that looks out onto the square where I see him walking. I take a step back, I don't want him to see me, he doesn't need to know how I feel about him. I opt for the illusion and hear myself thinking about the possibility of turning my simple day-to-day worries into a surreal world, inspired by reality. A reality that looks like that of so many, a shared experience. An experience that I want to enrich, make more beautiful. Wishing and visualising because my fantasy tells me something about my reality. Dreaming about how I wish things were, even though I am not sure how I want things to be, unable to believe that happiness really exists. Luck has always seemed fleeting, too rapidly chased away by cumbersome situations. Situations that cross my path to teach me something, giving me a tool to use for my future. Life lessons, I often find them exhausting. Life starts at forty. My eggs all but gone, my body confused. For some time now my biological clock hasn't ticked that loudly any more. Technically it is still possible, but I am not very technical and I no longer wish to have a copy of myself. I find it far too difficult to be such a copy myself. The daughter of a daughter. Too much recognition, too many frustrations unintentionally impressed upon every cell of my body. So much to process. Incomprehension and comprehension hand in hand while I extricate myself with ups and downs from the woman who gave me life, discovering my own individuality, larded with bits of my mother. For as long as she lives her daughter, her child, even now that the first signs of becoming old have entered my life. Forty; not so much ticking any more, but still a lot of pounding going on and my imagination gladly leads me away from the loneliness and unanswered desires when I see him crossing the square. I look at him with passion and suppressed desire. I imagine him more beautiful, taller and kinder. His brown eyes are blue and his hair full of curls, natural curls, naturally. His designer clothing is casual and his shiny shoes are a little grubby. His fingers are long and slim but his beautiful big nose is still the same. I love big noses, and consider myself strange as a result of this, a stranger to myself. My desire incomprehensible, but it doesn't matter. I don't want to think about that, don't have to think about that now. I watch him turning around and walking towards me, I want him to, and smile timidly at him. He looks at me and sees me for who I really am. My emerald green eyes are brown and my ginger hair is dark blonde. He is now with me, looking at me, drowning in my eyes. He caresses my long hair, very gentle and cautious, holding my face in both hands, gently kissing my forehead. His eyes slowly glance over my body, provocatively, using his hands to discover every secret part of me. An electric energy runs through my body. He touches me inside; I'm happy, but also scared. My feelings quite vague because I actually thought I was in love with someone else. That other person, so unapproachable, and now so near, becoming him. I push aside my confusion. He is there for me now. He thinks I am beautiful; passion clearly visible in his eyes. Slowly he opens the buttons of my blouse. I like that, the tension grows. I let him continue, go far, very far and now I am naked. I shiver and he puts his arms around me, says everything is fine, kissing my earlobe, my neck. I carefully push my shy body against his. He reacts, no longer hiding his agitation, with a hoarse voice, whispering sweet words that I don't understand. It doesn't matter. His experienced hands search for the contours of my body. As if in a trance my hands discover his attractive naked body. His chest, neck and shoulders, thick dark hair, straight back and firm buttocks. He is not tall, but very masculine. I enjoy the touching. Suddenly my body is no longer in line with my head and an excited feeling overwhelms me. The caressing more intense, our bodies hot. He is breathing heavily and his warm mouth explores my most sensitive spots, visibly excited, tangibly intense. I feel the heat, the heat of desire. Something is not right, but everything is very ok in my lower belly, further down, deep below, very deep. I am afraid of myself because it feels so safe. Frightened of the confusion because I know it should be different. He has become him and I imagine that I love him. I want it to continue, for ever. Time stands still. Reality blurs. He is tender but without doubts, knowing what he does and must do for me to create my ecstasy. We do it almost in secret because it happens only in my head whereas my body automatically leads its own life. My breathing intense; wetter ... everywhere ... Enjoying the uncontrollability of the moment in which I imagine him in me, melted together into one, which we were already anyway. He in my head, now also in my body, pushing away the loneliness. I love him the way I should. Something is happening, something is moving, I withdraw myself, the curtain back into place, caught by him.

Beyond love

Maybe I can do it, make myself happy. I'm eating a small tart in a café filled with old tarts, almost feeling a bit of a tart myself, I might become one tomorrow. Thoughts filling my head whilst I look out of the window, reminded of my own loneliness by a homeless person on a bench. Abandoning his soul while he lives the essence of his life, without understanding. His loneliness frighteningly clear so that I have to look the other way. A homeless person holding up a mirror but I don't want to see the reflection. I do it anyway, confronted by a stranger with my subconscious fear of being alone, the unknown familiar. Recognizing a silent desire to share a part of my life, attracted by a human being who I gradually allow into my life. Wanting to give and receive but not being able to clearly indicate that vague border that seems so important. Reluctance because of the fear of having to lose something that feels so good, an unbearable thought. Frightened to enjoy the freedom of being together, maybe because it is too beautiful, it's easier to be a vagabond. But not like the homeless man, his sad passing mentioned in the newspaper, forcing me to be aware.

* * *

There was also something else in the newspaper. A contact ad, my contact ad, written in a moment of desperate loneliness mixed with a powerful desire for adventure, and self-confidence that wasn't always so obvious. A hotchpotch of letters in a space of two by five centimetres containing my life and wishes. 'Attr.full.fig.fe.search.f.attr.male.' I was surprised by the amount and normality of replies with the obligatory photo. Several dates with different men were the result, not always hoping for it to continue with a second date. But then he came along. He was larger than I had imagined and strikingly attractive. The click between us seemed audible. I heard myself thinking … 'Hello handsome,' but I didn't know him. I was paralysed by the fear of rejection, a fear that had nothing to do with him, but everything to do with my past. An accumulation of parts of my past. He was clearly not perfect which I found attractive, hoping that he would accept my imperfections. A non-occasional meeting which moved on to my house. Fast, because it felt OK. Amusing conversation, a delicious meal and a mixture of body heat and feelings. Discovering myself in an unprecedented enthusiasm to explore with my tongue, making the unknown familiar. A recognition of feelings and actions, different from any time before. Because he was different. A large, strong, hairless body, which secretly made me slightly jealous. Long thick black hair resembling a native American Indian. He smelled of freedom and adventure, his mouth and hands experienced to satisfy. Our naked bodies felt good together; my prudishness dissipated by a powerful desire for more. I could feel the fast beating of my heart, my hands automatically finding their way to his warm back, firm buttocks and strong legs, seductive. Coming together with the promise of forever, chasing away time for a moment.

He was dangerously attractive and tasted so good that I wanted more of him. A silent desire because I didn't know where he was and what he felt when he thought about me, or perhaps not. Suspecting that he was someone who gets in touch when he has time and will only then want to experience me again, close by. For me so far away while I find myself unwillingly in that so typically female role, with a tendency to arrange my life around my telephone. Frightened of not being good enough. Scared that he would run into his soul mate, because maybe that is who I wanted to be, for a moment or for eternity. Frightened for his fears which I didn't dare take away because I understood them so well, or maybe it was only in my head. I felt attracted by his freedom, so recognizable. Attracted by the enthusiasm when he spoke about his passions. Longing for more, discovering him further, the promised intensity, love for life. I didn't want to change him, only myself. Letting go. He gave me some beautiful moments, but also sadness, which made me long for the loneliness which was more bearable when I only dreamed of him. Now still, intangible feelings caught in my heart, I don't understand them, I do understand them. Memories of moments when he looked into my eyes and told me that I was sexy which intensified the feeling when we kissed. He more attractive to me than I to him. In love with his being different, with his unreachability, because deep down inside I was too scared of not being alone. Loneliness perhaps too familiar to be able to live without.

Like the homeless man. I learned to deal with the feeling of rejection. Having to move on, beyond the pain. Prepared to learn, to live, to teach, especially myself. I could live with his understandable unreliability, small promises not complied with, now unimportant. And when he escaped from his problems, I forgave him that he saw me as a problem. Putting my memories in a rucksack where they will remain until they no longer suit me. Keeping myself going by following my heart, leading me away from blame, filling me with a different type of love, because it is better for me. He is in my heart, that heart that is big enough. Every now and then I put him back in my head, now still too often, but that will become less. Leaving him as he is, so that I can become who I am, in the future or only in memory. Beautiful because time does not exist. The unknown familiar. Beyond love.

Chat

It was 11 o'clock at night and his partner had just gone to bed. He often used the late hours to surf the net, opening his Skype account to chat with people all over the world. It was exciting; some women approached him unashamedly free in word and action. He had become addicted to it. His girlfriend had no idea of this surreal life which he nevertheless experienced as a form of love. She trusted him completely. He did feel guilty, because he knew that she would find his behaviour terribly offensive, but the urge was too strong. He couldn't resist it. In those late hours he built up a forbidden world, a web of lies which became his reality. The ladies he chatted with not even aware of his real situation. Unaware of the fact that his single status, his job as a photo-journalist, his life in a remote house in the north of Scotland, in no way approached his reality, so similar to that of many others, his colleagues at the office his only social contact. Friends had disappeared, his social life was practically non-existent. He decided to go to bed early that evening, and started to close the websites he had just visited. Suddenly the bottom of the screen started flickering. Uninvited, she came into his life via the Skype-me setting on his computer.

* * *

'Hello ... wait a minute, I will explain that ... The H comes from my lower belly, the E from my heart region, the double L from my warm tongue and the O ... Ooooooh.'

* * *

He took fright, started to sweat, felt uncomfortable. Who was this? He took a close look at the small photo in the top left of the chat box. It did not show much more than a vague image of who she really was. The photograph was taken in a dark room with some candles. She had long hair and an oval face, a small chain decorated her neck, but the image was very vague. It made her mysterious, arousing him. He felt naughty and knew he was walking on thin ice, forbidden ground. He went to the bedroom where his partner was in deep sleep, convincing himself that he could not be caught. He poured himself a glass of whisky and went back to his computer. Strange that he did not know exactly what she looked like. Good to keep it that way.

* * *

She did not promise him that she was wearing a sexy tiger-print outfit; after all, he might not even think that tiger-print outfits are sexy. She told him what he wanted to hear. She knew that taste differs and it wasn't important to her how he saw her, so she vaguely described what she was wearing. A tight revealing dress and shiny stockings with suspenders and stilettos.

* * *

The images already in his head. He knew the dress was black with a lace border, he liked that, and the shoes were of a beautiful, expensive, quality leather with silver stiletto heels. The stockings, black and transparent in a tasteful way, went up all the way to the exciting lace suspenders. Tonight, just for a moment, she was entirely his. He thought she was beautiful, even more so because he would never meet her, never knowing who she really was. To him she had the skin colour that aroused him, the body that heated him, the mouth that made him go red in the face, eyes which he wanted to stare into. She was his muse while he was hers, but he did not want to think about that. Not knowing her meant that he could create her.

* * *

She gave him some incentives which he could mix with his private world. Her hands were sensitive, skilfully applying oil over warm parts of a body, her body; the body that excited him, his world, his fantasy. He could guide those hands and let them do those things that he enjoyed. She asked him to lead her.

* * *

He let her hands caress her beautifully shaped body. Carefully those hands opened the zip on the back of her silky dress. She slowly took if off, not wearing anything underneath; he knew that she was completely naked apart from the stockings. He knew that she caressed herself as never before, inspired by him. He read her mysterious arousing words which came to him through his screen, he imagined her voice. It was a sensual, somewhat dark voice. He fell in love with the hope, the expectation, the fantasy and the inaccessibility, aroused.

* * *

She wanted to take him along in her world and told him a story from her memory, to stimulate him, to confuse, and to let him understand even less of who she really was. 'I'm sitting in an age-old garden, in the shade. It is terribly warm and a pigeon coos with excitement. If I allow the sounds to get through to me one by one it becomes pleasantly confusing. I will take you along. If you listen carefully, you can feel it. Singing birds, a moped which, for a moment, drowns all sounds, vague voices, a chain-saw in the distance. Feet running away on wooden sandals. Rustling leaves in the trees and my heavy breathing. I am naked and know that only you can see me, here in this garden. Caressing myself, opening myself up for intense feelings which I will experience on my own.

'A late evening sun warms me, healing ... the wind is lovely, like a gentle balm. I will do what you want me to do in this garden, with the body created by you, my hands guided by you, I am yours, just for a moment! Teasing.'

* * *

He became more and more excited and entangled in a web of desires, lust and frustration about the impossibility of reaching her, of really making her his, of really being able to feel her body. He loved getting her attention, loved his attention for her, but deep down inside he also felt lonely, indescribably alone in his fantasy which could never substitute reality.

* * *

She had enough, getting bored, feeling tired, with no satisfaction. She was lonely as well. In her forbidden world, a world which she could only share with virtual visitors, strangers, who were unable to unravel her mystery. She got up and walked to the mirror, took off the glittery blue dress, kicked off her red pumps and went to the toilet in her black boxer shorts. She stroked her face and chin and realised that by now the stubble was quite visible and she knew that she could never be the woman she pretended to be. Not even knowing whether that was really what she wanted, what he wanted, becoming a man again. He took off the wig and the false eyelashes, washed the heavy make-up from his face and shaved it before he went to the bedroom where his wife was in a deep sleep. One last time he walked to the computer. His hands slowly moved in the direction of the mouse, moving it to the little cross in the top right-hand corner of the chat box ... Click!

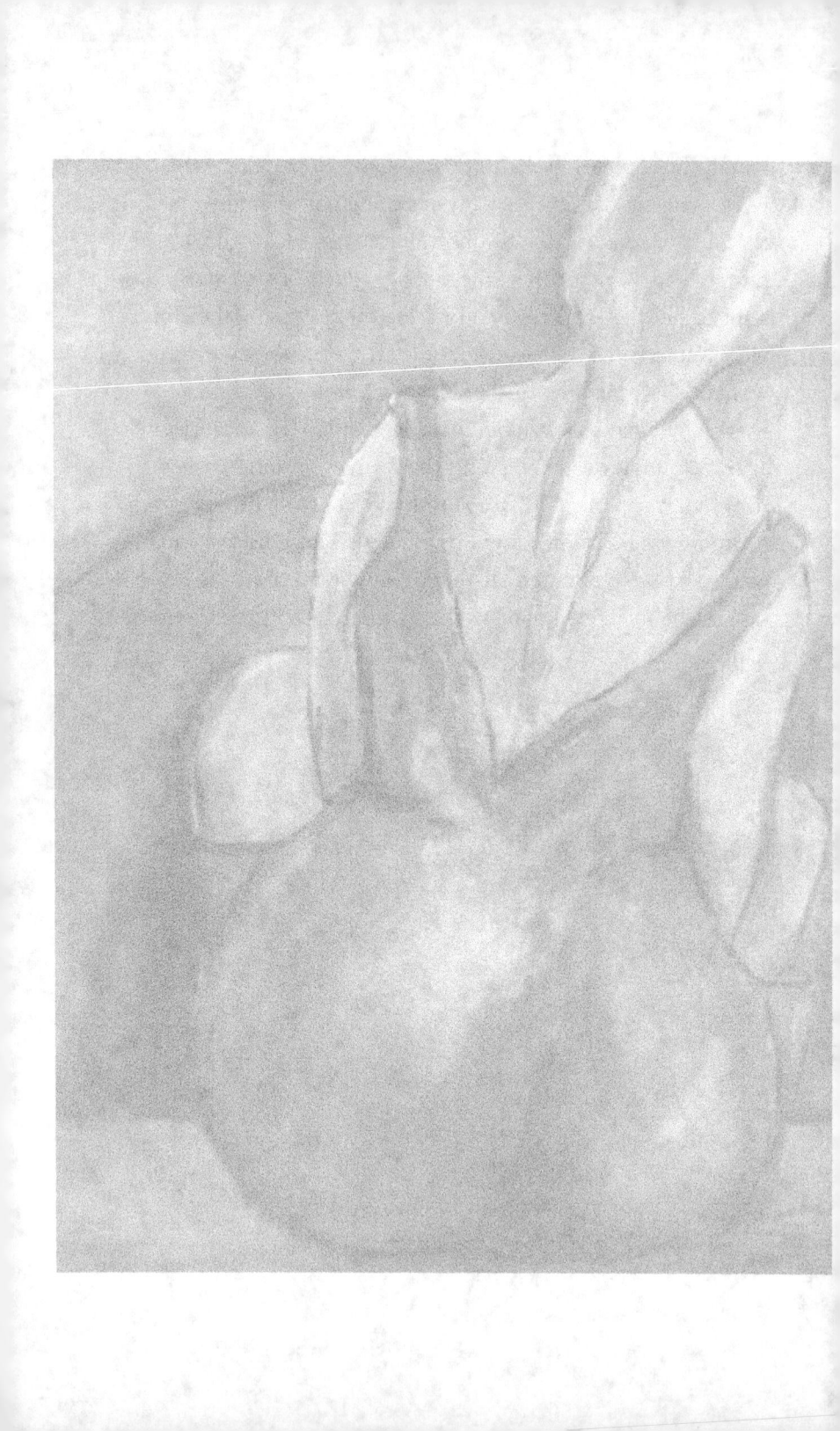

The lamp post

I am a lamp post and you might not expect it, but I am alive. I can think, feel and observe, and that is what I often do. Just staring at the world from above. At night I shine my light over everything that happens around me which gives me a very special feeling. Energy is flowing through me; a powerful tingling warms me deep inside. I am a lamppost in a shopping street surrounded by many bars and restaurants in the centre of a large city. From early in the morning until late at night people come and go. I recognize a lot of faces, I like that, it makes me feel at home. I am of course part of the daily routine, always more or less the same, and yet each day is different.

Every morning the restaurant on the other side of the street opens its doors at ten o'clock sharp for early customers. Ladies with grey and pink perms, chatting sociably, enjoy their coffee and apple cake at the table in front of the large glass window overlooking the street. At 11 o'clock at night the tired manager of the restaurant closes the doors after a day of comings and goings. I like observing all this. The other cafés in the street are also filled with customers, from early morning till late in the evening. At night, I often come to their rescue and give them support when they are in a state of drunkenness. I don't mind that, I like to be important, but I do feel a bit sad that I am not really appreciated, just taken for granted, a simple object. But I am not that ordinary, I am very sensitive and sensual. Energy flows through me, energy is life. I am alive. Especially at night. Then I shimmer with excitement and am electrically charged, my head then starts glowing and lighting up. I am a straight pole and rather stiff, a symbol of manhood. My stiffness sometimes bothers me. I would love to hang my head down every now and then, looking at everything close by. Or be a paving slab for a while, looking up, instead of just looking down, especially in the summer! Simply doing nothing, just lying there, lazy, watching beautiful women walking all over me. Having a peek under the short skirts of young ladies, unnoticed. I often watch those beautiful briefs in the shop window of the lingerie shop next to the restaurant across the street. Beautiful briefs with silk bands and flowers. Sometimes really small with only a tiny piece of fabric and a thread. That is what I would love to see, where those little threads disappear into. Secretly picturing that, cotton strings with tiny flowers between round or sagging buttocks under happily moving skirts of all kinds of fabrics. It arouses me.

You might not see it, but that does not mean that it doesn't happen; electricity rages through my pole. Do not underestimate my appearance. There is a little hatch in my pole. That is where it all happens, where the titillation and excitement always starts. What nobody seems to realize is that I actually exist, that I have feelings. You can also touch me and if you are very quiet you can actually feel my tension.

* * *

Tracey walks out of the café, a little tipsy, that is when she sees me. It is almost as if I am talking to her. I call her. She feels a little dizzy, incapable of controlling her curiosity. She walks up to me, looking around to make sure nobody is watching her, because it is of course slightly crazy. She carefully puts her flat hand on my pole, then, a little overconfident, she puts both her hands around me at the height of her head. She closes her eyes and concentrates on what she feels; it is a nice feeling. A little cold, yet tingly. She pushes her lower body against mine. Then she puts one of her legs around my post, pressing her cheek against my cold exterior. She stands there for quite some time and I become warmer and warmer. She now tries to feel the energy flowing and notices that I take possession of her. She feels her lower legs, her thighs and how the energy reaches her pelvis, warming her inside and making her heart beat faster and faster, her breathing more intense; she starts panting. No longer in control of herself she notices the sensual tension in her limbs; excited, drops of sweat bead on her face. She carefully pushes her body against me and slowly moves up and down, her g-string with the little pink flowers rubbing exactly the right spot, creating an extra-sensual desire between her legs. The world around her becomes blurred, her lower body moves in shocks, full of desire and lust.

* * *

I was there for her. I enjoy her. I see how flushed she is in her face and want to give her even more of what I have in me. I sense her warmth and for a moment I shine more brightly. I fill her with my energy which now changes her body, through an uninterrupted flow, into a tornado of emotions.

* * *

She is completely lost in this moment of pleasure and cannot suppress a slight groan, not even wanting to. She feels light, lit up by me. She smiles and opens her eyes, suddenly aware of her surroundings. Her lips wet, a small blob of saliva glistening in the corner of her mouth which she, in shock, tries to hide from the laughing crowd on the other side of the street ...

The green pea

When I swept my balcony to enjoy the late spring sunshine I suddenly saw it. A green pea. I wondered how it had ended up on my balcony, very strange. It was a bright green, smooth, incredibly firm, rather large pea. I could not bring myself to throw it away. I was attracted to it by an unstoppable inner force and felt a strong desire to sit on it. I decided to follow my intuition. It was quite difficult, because I didn't want to flatten the pea. I carefully manoeuvred my well-shaped buttocks in such a way that the pea could carry my body. It was a strange sensation; a sensual feeling overwhelmed me. There I was, enjoying the sun and with a tantalizing sense that something unusual was about to happen. With my head leaning back against the wall I felt how the sun heated my body. Suddenly there was a voice. A hoarse, exciting voice. I took fright and looked around, but I only saw a butterfly. It was beautifully coloured, in shades of red, orange and brown, a large male butterfly. Macho, strong, but at the same time vulnerable and sensitive. The hoarse voice started to talk to me.

'Wow, you are so beautiful, and you smell so nice ...' I closed my eyes to enable myself to absorb the words spoken with that lovely voice. 'Your body is shining so sensually in the sun ... your full lips, invitingly moist. You are like an exotic flower.

Provocative, a little dangerous. I want to look at you, touch you with my thoughts, taking you with me in my fantasy. Let me guide you to the greatest delight.' I decided to surrender to the sun and the butterfly and I listened to the sweet, sultry words which were scattered over me. Like a tingling rain, begging for action. I started caressing myself. My slim fingers gently touched my face. I kissed the back of my hand and took my fingers in my mouth, one by one. The damp heat aroused me. I caressed my nostrils, my cheeks. My hands found their way to my neck and from there to the buttons of my blouse. I opened them, slowly. Suddenly the soft, gentle sound of violin music emerged from a rose bush, dreamily penetrating my ears. I took off my blouse and felt how the sun became aroused by me and started to shine even more intensely. I opened the front closure of my bra which imprisoned my excited breasts. They willingly let me caress them. Making small circles, gently pushing, provocatively slowly, in the direction of my sensitive nipples. I heard how the butterfly whispered sweet words into my ears. 'You are so beautiful, enjoy yourself, surrender to self-love. Free yourself and be yourself.' I took off my shoes and opened the zip of my skirt and took it off, impatiently. I massaged my feet. The sun and the butterfly watched, shimmering with excitement whilst I took off my briefs. I felt the force of nature and just for one moment it was completely silent, the air filled with electricity. I started to tremble all over, my hands following its roundness. Then I lay down on my back, rhythmically massaging. I was extremely aroused and felt the searing sun and the sensual stare of the butterfly. Next to me there was a large glass of sparkling ice-cold water. I wet my lips with some of the water and then carefully poured the rest on my shiny, sweaty breasts and belly. An even greater excitement filled me. My fingers greedily found their way to my warmest spot and I hungrily opened myself, feeling the warm beating inside and while the sun and the butterfly looked on, I allowed myself to come ...

Then I relaxed, relishing this special sensation. The sun continued to cast its rays and the butterfly disappeared over the horizon. Satisfied, I took one last look at my middle finger ... it had a tiny golden crown ... my own little prince!

Online dating

Just as I am about to cancel my subscription with the online-dating agency I notice the message in my inbox. 'Your profile has been visited!'

I decide to read the profile of the person behind the message and receive a list of likes, habits, wishes and other useless information about you. I imagine what your thoughts were when you read the words that I had entered in various languages about six months ago, not even remembering them myself.

I have to conclude that you were not impressed because you have not used the option to send me a 'wink' or an email trying to get in touch with me. Maybe you were put off by the fact that I live far away, or maybe you don't like the sound of my animals. I am left guessing, wondering why I even care, but your profile is so vague that it leaves open too many possibilities. They could be good. I try to discover some recognition in the small photo in the top left corner of your profile, but the Vaseline haze covering your photo doesn't give away any clues.

It reminds me of Mother Nature's fine ways when we suddenly find ourselves confronted, around the age of forty, with diminishing eyesight, so that we see each other in a constant blur, hiding the wrinkles and brown skin marks which have appeared out of nowhere.

I am intrigued by you and wonder what you will be like. A smoker, not sporty, but a health-centre lover, says the information. It puts a curious smile on my face. Who are you? Divorced, three years older than me, father of one child not living with you? You're a musician, which could mean anything from a brass band to a symphony orchestra, and you have an interest in a variety of music, including metal/hard rock and chamber music. Chamber music? That reminds me of elevator muzak, filling me with the fear of getting stuck in a lift with a sweaty individual who screams out in sheer panic, trying to escape the claustrophobic situation. But I could of course be lucky, it could be you.

We don't know each other but the attraction is obvious at first. We both need to go to the fifth floor. You push the button and the doors close with a soft sigh. You seem to enjoy the music and are totally unaware of my dislike. The lift starts to move, but not for long. With a loud metal bang we stop and the sound of music disappears. We look at each other. You can see the panic in my eyes and talk to me with a warm, gentle voice, trying to help me to calm down. I don't want you to smell my fear nor for you to discover that I want to scream my way out of this claustrophobic place.

It is warm in the elevator … suffocating, and I cannot breathe. I have to take off my clothes and you help me. You open the buttons of my black blouse and slowly move it down my arms till it falls on the floor. I hear your breathing getting deeper. Your hands go to the zip of my black trousers and without taking your eyes off mine you open it, my trousers fall to the floor. You help me step out of them. Without asking you know that I want you to continue and you have no problem finding your way to the closure of my black silk bra. Slowly moving the straps down my arms, welcoming my breasts into your hands. Then you strip off my black silk briefs and gently take me in your arms.

I don't know why I trust you but I do. You manage to take away my nervous energy and I feel totally relaxed and protected in your strong arms. You soothe me and tell me that you are feeling warm as well. I take a step back so that you can take off your clothes. You rapidly strip off your shirt and jeans, uncovering your strong physique. The black hair on your chest looks soft and inviting. Slowly you take off your navy boxer shorts. Now both naked we observe each other's bodies and the sensual tension is very strong in the small space. You have to touch me and take me in your arms again, this time caressing my back, burying your nose in my hair, telling me that you want me. Your hands find their way to every round shape of my body, lovingly, full of greed. Your lips looking for my lips while you press your lower body against mine. I feel your interest rising and I move in waves, accommodating my body to yours. Our warm tongues play a game of recognition, teasingly. Without words we lie down in the bottom of the lift on the small pile of clothes. Every cell in my body wants you to touch me, feel me, both inside and out. Pheromones all over the place help create a passionate, intense moment of love-making ... I'm loved and love you back. It is natural, our bodies happy to be together, our minds becoming one ... totally losing track of time, together exploding in a private moment of ecstasy.

The music suddenly comes back on. The lift starts to move again. You help me to get up. We put our underwear in our pockets as we frantically get dressed, just in time for the doors to open, welcomed by a large crowd of people worried about our situation ...

But unfortunately you are not interested in getting to know me. Slightly disappointed I switch off my computer and go to bed.

Dream behaviour

I came from a different dimension. Feeling heavy, confused and yet warm and satisfied. I was still in bed and had the vague sensation of just having woken up from a strange dream. I had a good stretch and just for another moment I enjoyed the warmth of the duvet mixed with the fresh breeze in my face that came in via the open window. About ten minutes later I decided to get up, lazily dragging my legs over the edge of the bed, stroking my legs, realizing it was a good thing that I was not in the company of a handsome man. I straightened my messy hair and opened the curtains. Looking out of the window of my small apartment in the centre of my home town I saw two ducks standing in the car park. They seemed out of place just like me, moments later scared by a boy on a moped. Scattered apart, loudly chattering, almost crying and flying away not very elegantly. The flapping of their wings making a wooden sound. I wondered whether other people also carried around this much noise in their head. I could not escape from the surreal sentences and images which entered my mind uninvited. Oh yes, I had tried to stop them; had followed a meditation course, but dancing around while chanting mantras, to admittedly great music, in a room that was far too small, with people that I would normally not mix with, had not really been me. It made the stream of words in my head even more intense and crazy. Quite often I welcome my delusions, they amuse me. I always see more than there actually is. Every object, every person and every animal, without knowing, is surrounded by a dream world containing their present, future and past, interwoven, in that order. I can absorb that dream, my brain turning it into words, correct or incorrect, it doesn't even matter. I listen to it, look at it and sometimes even find it funny, often tiring, mostly only useful to kill some time. I went to the bathroom and took a warm shower. It didn't really wake me up; that was OK. Feeling a little lethargic, it was pleasant enough to let it continue, enjoying it. Time was on my side, no plans for the day so I went to the kitchen to squeeze some oranges for my morning juice. Suddenly I heard the sound of horses in a cobbled street. I vaguely realized that the noise was coming towards me, becoming increasingly louder. It was him. On a beautiful black horse with a long black mane and strong legs. He invited me to join him on the back of the horse. I saw his gorgeous body, with seductive skin to touch and eyes to drown in. His words expressed in a warm dark voice, caressing my ears. I decided to accept his invitation to come with him. Joining his wisdom, to teach him, learn from him. He reached out his hand to help me onto the horse. I felt his warm body and wrapped my arms around his waist, carefully pressing my body against his. My cheek leaning against his back, closing my eyes. The gentle, somewhat cool wind and the warming sun accompanied us. Sensing everything. The horse was supple and strong and carried us in a rhythmic cadence in the direction of the sea. We dismounted, took off our shoes and walked barefoot, the beach to ourselves. The air was clear and the sea rolled happily on the sand, the wind playing a joyful game with the gulls, killing time, waiting for fishing boats to come in, as every morning. We looked at each other, held hands and walked in silence. With restrained tension, with the unexpressed certainty of love. Enjoying the smells of nature, our bodies. Enjoying the sun and the wind, created only for us in that very moment. Walking towards a beautiful spot in the dunes with pampas grass waving in the wind like the slightly too long hair of a girl on a bicycle waiting in front of a traffic light on a windy day. A warm excited sensation overwhelmed me, I was trembling. The humid warmth of my body stimulated my senses. Careful, lively and at the same time also intense twinges found their way to my lower body. I was floating. His hand almost accidentally touched my buttock. We were both hit by an invisible electric shock. I was certain he would tell me that he loved me, even if that was not important to me, but he didn't seem to mind, just wanted to touch me, smell me. Burying his nose in my hair. Caressing my body, getting excited by the warm damp skin, exploring every tiny spot, kissing me. Enjoying my caressing hands. Longing for those hands on his back, massaging his abdomen, slowly, further down, teasing him, approaching his most intimate part. His body merging with mine, almost unnoticed thoughts becoming one. With respect, with admiration, with love and lust. Feeling how the wind played a sensual game with our nakedness. The grass calling us to lie down, becoming one, a dream expressed in a sensitive explosion ... in the dunes, the sea, the gulls, our bodies. Suddenly I heard the rustling pages of an open book, inviting us, slightly hidden in the dune grass. I picked it up. He was sitting behind me; I leant against his chest, protected, warmed. Reading the words which entered our heads via the white pages of the book. 'It was as if I came from a different dimension. I felt heavy, confused and yet warm and satisfied. I was still in bed and had the vague sensation of just having woken up from a strange dream ...'

Train stories

We are standing still. I am looking out of the window into a room. It is called a waiting room, you could also call it a watching space. A view into space. Not looking at anything in particular. A temporary shelter for the less fortunate. I see a woman in the space, she is sleeping and is about the age of my mother. I imagine that I can smell her. She is dirty, lying under some old rags. A crumpled-up brown paper bag containing a bottle stands next to her on the floor. I can't really see the woman, I don't need to, I already know that she is lonely. The children she never had have left her. Now accompanied by her cat on this last journey which is her life. The cat lies next to her, asleep, satisfied, partially under the old rags with a peaceful smile on his little face. Unlike the woman. She has had enough, sleeping is now a way out. At the moment she doesn't have to look for something to fill her rattling stomach, to moisten her dry mouth. Travelling away from reality in her sleep. Will she still dream? Dreaming of a normal life in the future? A house with a small garden where her cat could happily play with his dingy toy mouse without a tail. Perhaps she could even buy him a fluffy new mouse. And every evening cooking tasty food with fresh potatoes and vegetables from her former neighbour's garden, the neighbour that she had secretly been in love with her entire life. That neighbour who also liked her. She was sure about that because every Saturday he came, neatly polished in his best clothes, to drink a cup of coffee with her and he always brought a small bunch of flowers and some vegetables from his garden for her. It made her nervous, she wanted to hide in his arms, embracing and kissing him and maybe even a bit more. She tried to imagine that they both walked into her bedroom and took off their clothes and that he kissed her gently on her white skin that never saw a ray of sunshine. Caressing her everywhere on forbidden little spots. She tried to imagine that she loved that, but never really dared to give in to her fantasy and for this reason, to get a little courage, she kept walking back and forth from the kitchen to the room, secretly drinking small glasses of gin in the kitchen followed by some peppermint candy, so that he wouldn't smell the alcohol.

In her dreams there was no gin. In her dreams she was a self-confident woman who seduced the neighbour into living their lives together. Was her dream more beautiful than reality? Aren't dreams always more beautiful than reality? How can something that is intangible be beautiful? The brown paper bag with the bottle falls to the floor, some spirit drips out of it. The cat takes fright and looks up, but the woman is in a deep sleep.

* * *

My eye is caught by a priest walking past on the platform. He is pulling along a large black suitcase. A large red bow, tied to the handle, happily dancing along to the rhythm of the walking priest. He gets on a train. I wonder why he attached the large bow to the top of his suitcase. Maybe he has been on a family visit to Foligno in the heart of Umbria in Italy, now on his way to Rome where he will try to forget the days that he has just passed, knowing deep down inside that it was a little indecent. With a smile on his face and with a naughty feeling he thinks back to the moment he met her again after 35 years. She was now married and had returned to her native village near Foligno for a visit to her sister. He recognised her immediately and saw the recognition in her eyes. Her smile just as sweet as when he saw her last, remembering her kind face with the large red bow loosely tied in her beautiful long black hair. He had processed the pain of the impossibility of their love. Their love, forbidden even now, but this time for other reasons. He didn't think that he could live without her. Both 15, old enough to recognise true love. But he came from a good family and she from a poor background. His family sent him to a strict boys' boarding school in Rome, which was managed by priests. Father Gianni was a kind, good-natured man, prepared to listen for hours on end to the words of the broken young man and without intention he ended up inspiring him to go into priest-hood. And now, the last day of his family visit, he saw her. As if in a trance they walked towards each other and suddenly the years seemed to disappear. Without words he took her hand and in silence they ran through the narrow streets leading to his father's house. He knew that his aunt and sister had gone out for the day and invited her into the large, dusty-smelling living room with the old pieces of furniture and the large open fire. They only had eyes for each other and he carefully put his arms around her and pulled her towards him. He could smell her delicious fragrance and feel her soft skin when he buried his nose in her thick grey hair. Time seemed to stand still while he carefully pulled her body closer to his. He felt the contour of her breasts through her floral dress. She caressed his back and first gently kissed his cheek and then carefully kissed his mouth. With hesitation they opened their mouths so that their tongues could meet. They caressed and kissed each other for a long time. Then they heard the keys in the lock of the front door. They rapidly straightened their clothing and she opened her bag and took out the large red bow. They shook hands with smiles on their faces, a careful embrace and a brief kiss on the cheek. He accompanied her through the hall to the front door. She then affectionately tied the bow to the handle of the large suitcase waiting in the hallway, ready for his return journey. Back to reality.

* * *

Where the train starts moving. I am sitting in seat 84 and look at seat 85. The number a little worn out. Once seat 85 was a sturdy and luxurious part of a first class train compartment. Now second class. I take a closer look. The grey upholstery has become dreary. Stains ingrained into the design. Stains have changed into design. Everything looks dirty. I imagine tiny flags coming out of the seats. Flags from Denmark, Sweden, Italy, the Netherlands, Spain, Morocco ... from almost all the countries of the world. They wave. The flags are held by tiny hands. The hands of millions of bacteria which have multiplied in the course of years in the upholstery.

* * *

The seat doesn't mind. He has already offered his support to so many people. Old now, kind of dismissed by society. Spending his last days unworthy of a pension. He doesn't complain. It has been great. It all started in quite a chic way ... civilised bottoms in neat women's suits of excellent quality, with a pleasant light odour which he very much enjoyed. Proud to be a support for distinguished ladies and gentlemen. Everything very discreet. Year after year. But a few years ago he was downgraded. Now a second class seat. Especially in the beginning it was quite shocking. Round bottoms in far too short skirts. Especially in the summer he was astonished at the shameless exposing of undercarriages. But he got used to it, was less interested in what happened around him, slightly tired. However, he did wonder if those ladies realised what the willing bacteria that were housed in his upholstery did beneath those skirts. He tried not to think about it, but he knew it of course. And if you were very quiet you could hear the screams of joy. I listened and thought ... as soon as I get home I will have a shower!

Meditation

Desperate to stop the overpowering stream of thoughts in my head I join a meditation group. After herbal tea and interesting conversation with like-minded people, recognizable by their German sandals, we enter a large room, dimly lit by five candles and filled with a strong smell of incense and the sound of softly singing Tibetan bells. Beautifully draped veils create an Eastern atmosphere. We take our places and for the next hour we sit without speaking with crossed legs, five minutes enough to make me feel hugely uncomfortable. Afraid to move and con-vinced that the noise in my head is audible to others, I test the mind over matter theory by suppressing a sneeze. It works. Aches and pains remind me of parts of my body that I did not know existed while waves of the strangest thoughts fill my mind. I try to calm down, visualising images of nature. Thinking of trees with spring-green leaves and the sound of swallows so typical of a summer's day, I realize that I am not supposed to think at all ... A bit panicky I try to imagine my thoughts being blown into a beautiful bright red balloon, taken away into the distance by a gust of wind ... I watch it getting smaller and smaller and for a few seconds I manage to relax, even forgetting about the pain. But then my body makes a noise and I notice a blown-up feeling in my inner beauty, so craftily designed by God when she thought up the need to fuel up and excrete. In fear of letting go of an audible or inaudible 'bum-sigh', I tighten all the necessary muscles, feeling hugely uncomfortable, totally defying the objective of the meditation. I hold my breath and am glad that nobody can see my face which by now must surely have a purple shine to it, beads of sweat playing a teasing game on my forehead ...

Wow ... what was that? Someone is touching my knee, clearly not by accident. My brain goes into overtime wondering who would dare to put his hand on my body, now clearly moving in the direction of my inside leg. I know very well who is sitting next to me; I had a good look at him from the corner of my eye in the garden before the meditation, while sipping my hot tea from a colourful Moroccan glass. I was fascinated by the way he talked, with his strongly accented yet soft warm voice explaining his life abroad to a tall man with skinny legs and large feet with white toes sticking out of grey leather sandals.

I feel a cold shiver down my spine, afraid to move, desperately trying to listen to the silence in the room. My lively intestines miraculously calm down, my painful crossed legs all of a sudden sensually and sexually inviting, an inappropriate sensation fills my entire body, bubbling up from my lower abdomen to the top of my head. I want him to continue, here, now ...

I know he is attractive in an unusual way. His green smiley eyes stared into the world with knowledge. He looked safe, gentle and boyishly cheeky. I imagine that his chest hair erupts like an explosion from his lower belly into a cloud of grey curls. I feel his well-shaped hand moving up, getting dangerously close to my most intimate spot. I take a secret peek between my lashes and convince myself of the serious meditative state of the others present in the room. I cannot but surrender to his curious imminent touch, without a trace of doubt pushing exactly the right button, making it impossible for me to keep in a soft sigh. He moves over and I feel his warm tongue penetrating my mouth, with precision, hunger and passion gently forcing me to respond. His hand finding his way to my breast, gently caressing and alternating with a circling movement, his fingers aware of my growing sensitivity. Lust and passion rage through my body, filling my mind with unstoppable forbidden thoughts.

I know I need to put an end to this, interrupt the stream of images and words that create an unrelenting yearning, afraid that I won't be able to control myself much longer. Time no longer exists, I know I am getting dangerously close to reaching a climax and a slight panic tightens my heart …

Then there is a reprieve … saved by the sound of three Tibetan bells that signal the end of the session. I look around, people are stretching and yawning, totally relaxed with peaceful, almost angelic expressions, my neighbour clearly unaware of my secret thoughts. I pray nobody will notice the embarrassing rosy glow on my cheeks and I take a deep breath …

Once outside a smile adorns my face, welcoming the sound of silence in my head.

I'll be back next week.

Time

You know that time doesn't exist when you suddenly find yourself in the past, which feels like the present, when the sound of the wind or a smell throws you back in time. Different to a déjà-vu, I thought, when I found his photo between the pages of a long-forgotten book. The photo fell on the floor, I picked it up and gave it a quick kiss. I was back in his arms in the car on top of the mountain, that early morning in August. Time returned and feelings became a vivid memory, steadily, more colourful than they were. I held the photo in my hand and poured myself a glass of Chianti. Eros Ramazotti filled the room with his music; the words not important, I didn't really listen. I went to the sofa, sat down and closed my eyes ...

It was six o'clock in the morning. They'd feasted on my blood, it had woken me up. Extremely itchy tiny white lumps with a red edge appeared on my skin. Creams, sticks, sprays ... nothing helped. Nothing is perfect, not even summertime. I tried to concentrate on something else, on my surroundings, but the itching took over. Zanzare! It sounds so nice in Italian. Zzzzzzzzzzanzzzzzzzzzzzare. They obviously liked me, those Italian mini vampires. Small mosquitoes full of bad temper. Uninvited, secretly enjoying me, probably seeing me as an exotic little treat, this woman from Holland. I got up and walked towards the window which looked down on the square of the small village in Umbria. I slept in a large room in the age-old grand home of my best friend and a lively panorama welcomed the early morning. Dozens of swallows and other birds had taken over the square, moving their wings as if in a hurry, happily. I did not know where they were going, where they came from, but they were hopefully feeding themselves on a few zanzare, possibly filled with human blood, my blood. The air filled with the wooden sound of flying pigeons, echoing between the walls of the ancient houses around the picturesque square. Concentrating on the singing and flapping of the different birds the sound became pleasantly deafening. The church bell rang, as it did every morning at five minutes past the hour. I wondered but never asked why. I heard a car door slam and the buzzing of a fat fly too close by. Unable to sleep any more I decided to go outside for a long walk. A fresh cool breeze accompanied me, calming my skin. Except for an early farmer the old village was an oasis of peace. The morning smell gave me a feeling of well-being and gratitude. I was happy. Lost in thought I walked in the direction of the valley. Suddenly he was there, I didn't see him walking towards me, but his beautiful, almost Greek nose made up for everything. A striking nose, one of those I always fell for, depending on what else was attached to it. The words he said in broken English were futile, unimportant; I wasn't paying attention, distracted by his white teeth and wonderful friendly smile, so attractive, inviting. The beams of his smile touched my heart. I found him incredibly special. He was now standing very close to me, I could touch him, smell him. I looked into his eyes and was aware of a mutual glance of unspoken attraction. I felt a bit shy and scared to follow my dream, but he helped me. He came from Naples, calling me Rene, it sounded sensual from his mouth. He took my hand and we walked to his car; he held the door open for me and asked me to sit down. I didn't mind him touching me and needed some adventure, far away from my past and my future. I got in the car, allowing myself to be taken along in this moment of excitement as he sat down next to me. We drove up into the mountains. After ten minutes we turned up a narrow sand track in the forest, parking the car beneath a canopy of leaves. A green shadow covered our bodies. His pleasant voice spoke quietly and I enjoyed the warmth of those words which I didn't understand; it wasn't important, we spoke each other's body language. He started kissing me. First with some hesitation, sweet, then becoming intense which left me longing for everything and more. I took off his t-shirt and stroked his toned breast, the black hair spreading like a wave from his lower belly to just below the warm dimple in his neck, invitingly curling between my fingers. He took off my t-shirt and wrestled with the closure of my bra, briefly bringing us back to reality, aware of the small space with awkward obstacles. Enhancing the excitement. Soon we were both naked. The sensation of the possibility of getting caught by an early passer-by made the situation feel unreal. My hands caressed his soft but masculine skin and I smelled the fragrance coming out of his pores, arousing me. I felt how he touched and embraced my curves with passion, gently massaging his way to my intimate heat. It didn't take long for him to join me within, filling me with a sense of delight so recognisable yet never felt before. A feeling I could not give myself. The beauty of being together turned into an unforgettable memory. I was vaguely aware that birds were loudly trying to welcome the morning with their songs, sharing our passion in that very moment. We listened to it in silence, intimately holding each other, the windows of the car misted over.

Then we got dressed and he gave me a photo picturing him with a broad smile. It fell to the bottom of the car, I picked it up and gave it a quick kiss. He drove me back to the village which was still in a deep sleep, that Sunday morning in August ...

Now Sunday evening in January. My glass empty. I close the book in which my memory is stored for ever, leaving time behind.

Reality of dreams

A drowsy-looking young man directed her to a parking space on the ferry boat. An overwhelming stench of car fumes and the claustrophobic atmosphere made her rush upstairs to the open-air decks. She passed an attractive man. *Gosh I wouldn't mind him saving my life in the event of a sinking ship.* Suddenly her coat fell off her shoulders and was picked up by the man she had just passed. *Oh he is so handsome.* Happy smiling crinkles in an interesting face revealing a life lived to the full, he looked at her, amused because he saw her thoughts were seemingly far away even though her eyes were resting on his face. She flushed, thanked him and took her coat from him, accidentally touching his hand. A wave of excitement filled her lower belly. She smiled timidly and turned away from him, feeling uncertain about having to walk up the stairs in front of him, aware of her swaying hips. A sigh of relief escaped her lips when she arrived at the outside deck, but it was too cold to sit down so she went to the restaurant, sat at a small window table and ordered a salad sandwich and an orange juice. It was a bright autumn day and the sunlight created an impressive fairytale spectacle on the surface of the sea with seagulls showing off their freedom. There was beauty in everything and she enjoyed the moment of peace and quiet. She allowed her thoughts to dissolve away the view, replacing it with fantasies about the attractive man that she'd met earlier. She imagined him starting a conversation with her as she invited him to join her for a drink. They talked about dreams becoming reality, regularly touching each other's hands, seemingly casual. They both felt the attraction growing. There were no other people in the restaurant and she opened her blouse. She was not wearing a bra and took her breasts in her hands, gently caressing them. She saw that he became incredibly aroused. Playfully she allowed him a glimpse of her completely revealed breasts, licking her lips while they penetrated each others eyes.

'Is this seat taken? ... Would you mind if I join you?' A deep sensual voice woke her up from her thoughts. With a slight sense of disappointment she looked up only to discover that it was him, the man from her fantasy. She felt caught out and knew her cheeks were turning red but said: 'Of course not, please sit down.' It was as if he were with her twice, in her head and now here in the flesh and it was as if he knew, as if he could read her mind when he gave her a warm cheeky smile. He was extremely direct when he continued, 'I think you are exceptionally attractive; I just have to be in your company for a while.' She realised this whole situation was very unusual, but it also felt okay and they went with the flow of the moment, talking about the very subject she had just been fantasising about. There was no need to know his name and he was not curious about hers. They admired the amazing view of the rough sea, the sensual play of the sun, talking about the beauty of people, the sensitivity of the soul and the excitement of a forbidden love. He observed her every move, her smile, her voice as it became deeper and more sensual. She welcomed his attention and went along in this foreplay of words, leading to a moment that was unavoidable and very much desired by them both. The excitement took on a visible form and she started wiggling on her chair, her body slightly shaking. She felt the pounding of her blood in her lower body. He saw it, grabbed her hand and pulled her up. Without talking they walked to the outside deck. It was deserted, the few passengers preferring to seek cover inside the ferry. They walked to a small space behind the wooden benches where they could lie down, sheltered from the view of other passengers, but in view of the sun, wind and sea-gulls. The sound of the waves against the steel body of the ship and the monotonous drone of the engine in the background of their perception. They spread their coats on the steel floor and lay down on them. She saw his greed, his passion for her, greeting it with a soft touch of her lips which was then followed by an intense exploration of their tongues. She sighed while responding to his warm and lustful kissing and smelled his aftershave, a masculine scent mixed with a hint of fresh sweat. His gracefully shaped hands gently but determinedly found their way under her shirt, touching her breasts, instinctively massaging her belly. He skilfully took off her shirt and opened the zip of her jeans, taking them off together with her briefs in one confident move. She was naked and incredibly aroused; impatiently she watched him take off his clothes and welcomed his warm strong body against hers. Gasping for breath she heard his warm voice whispering, 'Let yourself go.' She did, happy for him to take her, take her to another world. The excitement almost audible, exhilaration from the threat of other passengers discovering them making love to the rhythm of the waves. Making love the way it should be made, turning her fantasy into a sparkling reality. Their bodies satisfied, they dressed and walked back into the restaurant hand in hand. The loudspeaker made an announcement that the ferry had docked in England. Passengers were allowed to go to the car deck. They said goodbye with one last kiss. The reality had been far greater than she could ever have dreamed.

Mars and Venus

His marriage is at stake, he can almost surely forget his hedonistic role as a lover and it is not inconceivable that he will run into big problems at work. People had seen them together. He greeted Linda, the secretary, nonchalantly and did not want to show her that he felt caught out. His head full of excuses. 'I gave her a kiss to thank her, because she helped me with ... we are just friends ...' He had everything going for him. Married to a kind, attractive woman: Vera, his buddy, his friend and intimate partner. A son, Kevin, 12 years old, in whom he could recognise himself. A sweet and gorgeous mistress, who was independent enough not to want him to play a large role in her life, except to be the only one other than his wife. A great job with a dynamic company. Of course he knew that he was playing a dangerous game; he lived for the game, but he did not suspect that it would become his life. Oh he was such a jerk ... that of all people he had allowed Thea, the wife of his boss, to take him by surprise. He should have been smarter. Fact is, men are different from women. He remembered reading about that at some point. Men and women depicted as beings from different planets. It somehow made sense. Women always want to explain everything, understand everything and talk about everything ... He knows that Vera will not be able to understand that he really loves her, wants to share his life with her for always, cannot live without her. His family means everything to him. But that he nevertheless still feels the need to have a mistress. That says nothing about her, nothing about their relationship and also nothing about that mistress. He meant no harm and did not intend to be disrespectful. He still believes that his 'what the eye does not see, the heart does not grieve' way of doing things is not bad. However he should not have been this reckless and should have known better, realising that he had everything already and therefore could also lose everything. Thea had asked him whether he could give her a lift to a reception for the promotion of a new product at the company where he worked. That was not uncommon. Her husband was on a business trip abroad and he as his deputy also had some social responsibility. At five o'clock in the afternoon he picked her up at the gate of the large white villa in one of the upper-class districts of Zeist. She looked amazing, wearing a smooth, revealing, silky, soft-green dress with golden embroidery. Her deep décolleté dress revealed nothing but stimulated his fantasy. He opened the car door for her. She smiled at him provocatively and pulled up her skirt unnecessarily high above her knees while she stepped into the car, showing him her well-shaped legs, enclosed in subtly elegant fishnet stockings and black pumps with stiletto heels. She looked exciting but nevertheless exuded an elegance that was absolutely suitable for a business reception. They did not speak much during the short drive to the office, but he could smell her suggestive perfume, slightly too intrusive to be unaffected by it. The tension was tangible. He parked his car as usual in his reserved parking space, helped her out of the car and together they walked towards the building. It was busy in the hall, full of guests who were welcomed by the staff and accompanied to the reception area. She walked up the stairs in front of him to the restaurant on the first floor. He could not keep his eyes off her round swaying buttocks, so clearly visible under the smooth fabric. She was so damned attractive. The room was already filled with guests and employees and the environment was rather formal. He did not notice much of it, totally absorbed in their sensual game and the glance she gave him, revealing her intention. The subtle licking of her lips with the tip of her tongue. The way she picked a little bit of fluff from his jacket, seemingly accidentally, gently, yet unmistakably rubbing her breasts against his arm. The business reception, normally a boring obligation, had another dimension. It seemed as if they were the only ones present in a prohibited world. The surroundings became somewhat surreal. He was convinced that nobody was paying any attention to either of them. They went far, much too far, but clearly nobody was bothered by it. After a few glasses of champagne and a superficial chat with some guests she went to the toilet. He followed her after a few minutes, knowing that she would wait for him. She pulled him into the disabled toilet (in the ladies) and closed the door. He smelled her warm fragrance. Wrapped his arms around her, caressed her naked back and then downwards. He kissed her behind her ear, nibbled on her earlobe, her neck. She willingly let him until their lips found each other. Violently kissing and intensely caressing. He felt the fast beating of his heart and the fast beating of her heart through the thin fabric of her dress. Insolently he grabbed her buttocks and pulled her against him. She was greedy and excited, but just when he started to pull up her skirt she pushed him away, teasingly, with a smile and

opened the door of the toilet. She added a fresh coat of red lip-
stick to her attractive lips, straightened her dress, and smiled at
him via the mirror on the wall. Confused, he was left behind.
He told himself to remain calm and washed his hands and face,
combed his hair and nonchalantly entered the restaurant again.
After the reception they walked to his car together. And there,
in the view of customers and colleagues, he kissed her, just a
little too eagerly, on her cheek. He did not even realise it. Until
Linda the secretary greeted them. He felt caught out, but shook
that feeling off. He helped Thea into the car and they left in the
direction of her house. In the doorway they became more than
innocently intimate. Again he took her in his arms. Their
mouths found each other in a moment of ecstasy. Hands impatiently searching for the warmth of their naked skin. Wild, full
of passion. It took some effort to stop, not to go all the way,
while the light of the lamppost revealed their forbidden
meeting. She asked if he wanted to come in for a drink, but he
knew that once inside, he would not be able to stop himself and
would want to have her body, exploring her skin, devouring in a
passion which is so characteristic of a first 'forbidden' togetherness. Slightly remorsefully but firmly, he decided to refuse her
offer. He drove home in a fog.

Vera was waiting for him in the doorway. She was furious.
Linda had rung her. She thought Vera should know … ! The
bitch! He listened. 'All you men are the same. What were you
thinking … with the wife of your boss. Do you have any more
women up your sleeve?' She was right of course. In a flash he
saw his perfect world falling apart. He tried to defend himself,
to explain that he really loved her, could not live without her.
'Please Vera, I don't want to lose you …' He suddenly realised

that he could lose his job! He cursed himself, wishing that women did not exist. Vera shouted hysterically!! He felt drained so he got into his car because he no longer had the energy for a meaningless discussion. At that moment he did not care whether it was escapist behaviour. He had to think ... went for a long drive, to contemplate. Hey, why is that traffic light still on red? How long have I been waiting here for? Cute little thing by the way, that red-haired lady on the bicycle beside me. The light turns green; he takes one more look at her. Mmmm what a lovely sight, that small saddle sliding so cosily between her cheeks and legs ... I wish I ... !"

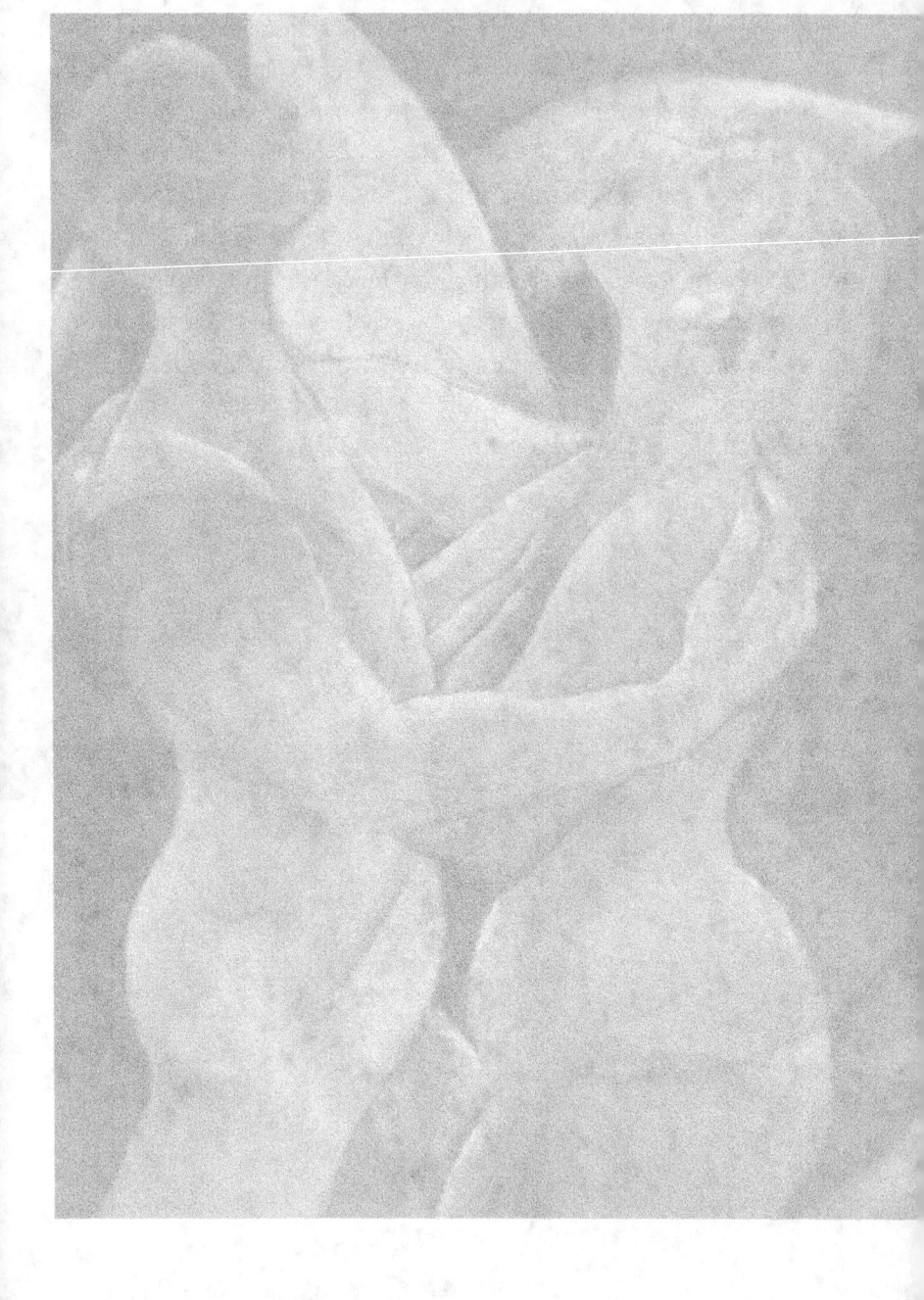

Massage in a bottle

The exhibition space is full of paintings of dubious quality which the artist tries to drown with a complicated explanation which nobody seems to be able to understand, but everybody feels they should admire. The atmosphere is strange, quite mad if you take it seriously. Modern classical music emanates from a flute and a piano, distressing sounds that frame the festive opening of the art exhibition. The flautist looks like a secretary and the pianist like a waiter. Ladies with grey perms pretend to like it but I don't believe them. It feels dishonest. I am sitting at the back of the room behind a woman with a tight boyish body sitting up straight on a wooden folding seat in her colourful handmade cardigan. A little tuft of hair, relishing the memory of sleep, unintentionally out of line on her head. Slightly too-trendy earrings dangling from her ears, tiny little balls attached to a chain of small beads that wobble to the sound of the music. I feel out of place and follow my instinct to leave the exhibition room. It is raining, but I welcome the fresh air. Then I see him, on the other side of the street, carrying a small, square, old-fashioned black suitcase, the leather slightly worn with a small piece of white fabric peeking out, flapping, calling out for help. Trapped. I watch in fascination. The fabric seems to be alive and I have an uncontrollable urge to save it. Amazed at this strange urge but wanting to follow my intuition I walk over to him. He is very attractive, sensitive and self-assured. I point at the suitcase and ask him if I can help. Astonished, but pleasantly surprised by my appearance he looks into my eyes. He has no idea why he is walking here in the pouring rain. However, he is vaguely aware of the suitcase that he is carrying but doesn't know its contents. He is curious enough to find out, together with me on this adventure, sensing that the sensuality of our encounter will become a fictitious reality. The tension tangible. In the distance we see a small church and decide to shelter there. We walk through the old overgrown graveyard in the garden next to the small church, stopping in front of the large dark brown wooden door, as if entry is forbidden, but then he carefully opens it and walks into this church, a church abandoned by God. I am right behind him. The church is run down but of a beauty which can easily be captured in words, but there is no need to explain, he understands the words without explanation. There is a vague smell of burned wood in the church, a smell of memory, of wood-stoves welcoming you when you walk through the narrow streets of a small mountain village during wintertime in some far-away country. The smell of cosiness and love, of excitement. Of good food and long evenings. Beautiful memories which could just as well be his. I want to warm him. The old wooden benches are no longer in a neat row. Suddenly he turns around and looks at me. I know that he can touch the depths of my soul. Emerging. I suddenly become a bit shy, he smiles at me. We look at the small suitcase now standing on the floor. We want to open it. The tension becomes more intense, pleasant. We carefully put the suitcase on a carved wooden bench. He slowly opens it and a silky satin sheet falls on the floor. At that moment the sun begins to shine and peeks inside through the broken stained-glass windows, scattering a colourful spectacle over the sheet. We spread it out over the bench and he picks up the brown paper bag which was also in the suitcase, containing some scented oil in a small bottle. A mixture of eucalyptus and lavender. There is also a message in the bottle. Written in beautiful elegant letters on an old yellowed note ... 'live in the moment, it is all you have'. I touch him and ask him to take off his clothes, lying down on the sheet. He looks at me, surprised, but he trusts me. With a nonchalant gesture, hiding his uncertainty so obviously that it makes me fall in love with him, he takes off his shirt. I am aroused and he notices it. Quickly he takes off his unpolished shoes and then his trousers and socks. Hesitating for a second before taking off his briefs, seductively. I look at his attractive naked body, giving me clear confirmation of my attractiveness to him. He lies down on his back on the satin sheet, his eyes closed. I can't keep my eyes off him and take my clothes off as well. Carefully I climb on top of him, using my body to rub his body, massaging it with the scented oil. Like a dancing snake moving up and down, discovering every angle of his lovely body, smelling his musky odour, kissing his neck, his ear, his mouth. His hands eagerly discovering me, watching and touching my curves, the rounding of my belly, my breasts. He tells me that I am beautiful and I recognize the desire in his eyes. I let him guide my body, his eyes hungry for more, his body and mind longing. The sun shines on our faces as we become one, enjoying our togetherness, an intimacy no longer in need of words. Time stands still whilst moving on. Love lasting the moment, living the moment. We are completely happy, convinced that God has just returned to the little church, smiling, knowing that we understood the message!

www.ingramcontent.com/pod-product-compliance
Lightning Source LLC
Chambersburg PA
CBHW060429260626
47161CB00005B/1855